Release (Liberação)

Volume 1 of A Lowell Story

Richard Hollman

ISBN:1468041509

ISBN-13:9781468041507

Dedication

For my wife Cindy and daughter Sarah for their indispensable help in developing this Story.
Para a comunidade Brasileira em Lowell e varios lugares tambem, pelo inspiração profundo.
To all Firsts, Seconds and Thirds everywhere.
To those who have lived, and continue to live, their own Lowell Stories
And to you, Dear Reader, for encouraging my behavior.

Chapters

Chapter 1

In which Beatrisa Meets a Strange Little Man

Beatrisa stood on the corner, clutching her coat against the chilly March wind, looking impatiently down Gorham Street for the city bus. It was very peaceful in this part of the city early in the morning, and might have been almost pleasant if you could ignore the dismal weather. There was some rush hour traffic on the streets, but it was too early and too cold for the derelicts and drug dealers to be out. At such times it was easier to appreciate the beauty of the hills, the waterways, and even some of the old buildings. This place was both old and new, in the sense that most of the old and rundown buildings were the first permanent structures that had ever been raised on this soil.

It was an odd city, really, and the closer you looked, the odder it seemed. Up the street was the empty space where St. Peter's had been torn down a few years back, leaving the street with the appearance of a demented, gap-toothed grin. Down the street was a remarkably beautiful brick building, an ornate little fortress with streets surrounding it on all sides like a moat, its dingy windows now crowded with dusty stacks of huge pots and pans and teetering cardboard boxes. Not far from here, a lovely section of the Western Canal passed in stately elegance through one of the poorest and most violent neighborhoods in the city. Indeed, it had been a poor and violent neighborhood for as long as the Western Canal had existed, which is to say, there had never been any other kind of neighborhood there. This was not a place where the exquisite and the shabby coexisted side by side. In this city, the exquisite and the shabby were one and the same, indistinguishable and inseparable, like a tree with an old vine deeply embedded in its trunk.

Where Bea stood, the smells of car exhaust from the street and garbage from the alleys battled with one another, each one momentarily gaining advantage as the wind shifted. But, as always, her mind was pulled away from these irritants by the steady roar of Pawtucket Falls, always dimly audible in the background. It was much more than a mere obstacle in the flow of the Merrimack River. Among other things, it was the reason for the city's existence, the source of the network of canals which still shaped the city, and the place where, many years ago, a sequence of events was launched which irrevocably transformed the entire nation. The nation had forgotten, but the canals still carried the memories along with their burden of slow-moving water. For Beatrisa, the sound of the falls always gave her the vague feeling that it had some profound significance, not only in the past but in the present as well.

As the drivers passed by on their morning commute, few noticed Beatrisa standing there. Short and round, with black hair and caramel-colored skin, she was an easily overlooked figure, mostly hidden by her hooded coat. If any passerby should catch a fleeting glimpse of her face, her preoccupied expression would not have invited further attention. This was her normal state: though she had been known to flash a dazzling smile on occasion, it was a rare occurrence. Her friends thought she was odd in this respect, and sometimes teased her about worrying so much. She assumed that they were right, and that she was strange, but it didn't seem like there was anything she could do about it. And at the present moment, the weather wasn't helping her mood.

Of course, winter was nearly over, and it wasn't as cold this morning as it had been just a few weeks ago, although her mother had complained about it, as she so often did. The weather certainly wasn't bad enough to justify taking the car. While Bea had a car and a license, she still walked or took the bus as much as possible. As everyone knew, every time you took your car on the road you risked getting into trouble. Her license was 'valid', as far as she knew, and the police here were mostly sympathetic, but it would only take one mistake, and a policeman in a bad mood, to bring down catastrophe on her and her family.

And she would need to renew the license this summer, too. Crap, that meant another trip to New Jersey, and another two grand under the table to those scumbags at the DMV. Her mother would be happy about it, at least. Mãe loved visiting her cousins and immersing herself in the Brazilian community there. For Bea, there was more than enough Brazilian community here in Lowell, and she didn't have any desire to go seeking out more.

It was a sour train of thought, but unavoidable on a cold day, waiting for the bus to take her to her job. Mãe didn't understand. It was all very well to work hard, keep out of sight and out of trouble, save a little money when you could, and pray for better times. But Bea was in a cage, along with the rest of her generation, and could not imagine ever being comfortable in it. For her, Brazil was a hazy memory of beautiful flowers, lively music and lots of anxiety at home. The Brazil in the posters at the travel agency across the street was more real to her than the Brazil of her own memories.

According to her mother, life there had been idyllic until her father died in a traffic accident, leaving the family with hardly any money, while the country was in the midst of a long recession. Her mother, like so many others at the time, obtained tourist visas for herself and her kids, and they boarded a plane for the US. They settled here in Lowell, where Mãe found work at minimum wage (or often less) to keep them going, and learned how to stay clear of the authorities after their visas had expired. She worked very hard, juggling two jobs, sometimes three, and sharing child care with neighbors. It seemed like an arrangement that could go on indefinitely, since there were always jobs available of this type.

Bea became aware of the cage as she made her way through the public schools in Lowell. She had picked up English quickly, and found school very easy. She was an exceptional student, earning her way into the most advanced courses, and particularly enjoying the math and science classes. This success brought her into occasional contact with the top students from the nearby, more affluent communities, and the gulf between them and herself was impossible to ignore. Their school experience was rounded out with extra-curricular activities, sports, music, travel, clubs of all kinds. They had college to look forward to, and a bright future was theirs for the taking. Bea could not afford to participate in any of the activities offered at her school. The best she could do was to spend as much of her school day as possible in the computer lab. College was out of the question. Her life during her school years was simple: she studied, helped out at home, went to church on Sunday, and spent time with her friends when she could. There was no bright future beckoning her. As intelligent as she was, as talented as she might be, as much as she was capable of accomplishing in this American culture which was more hers than Brazilian culture could ever be: without documents, the opportunities to use these talents would always be severely limited.

Things could be a lot worse, she supposed. Four years after finishing high school, some of her friends were cleaning rooms in hotels, or working in fast food restaurants, and had no prospect of ever doing anything more than that. The boys mostly ended up on house painting, construction or landscaping crews. The smart ones lived very frugally, and saved their money to become silent partners in those businesses. The stupid ones got drunk on beer and caipirinhas on Saturday night, ran traffic lights or drove too fast on the Connector, and quietly disappeared.

Bea's talent for electronics had been noticed by her high school teachers. One of those teachers, sympathetic to the predicament of the Brazilian students, had put her in touch with Rudy Foster, a Jamaican immigrant who owned a used computer store in the Lowell Highlands neighborhood. Starting in her senior year and continuing after she graduated, Rudy gave her a job in the back room, off the books, doing repairs, upgrades and software installs. It was a good arrangement. It would never occur to ICE to look for illegals in a business like that, and her presence there could be explained away in any number of ways, should it become necessary. The work usually wasn't very challenging, but it was occasionally interesting, and kept her in touch with the latest (or close to the latest) in technology. She could sometimes scavenge discarded hardware for her own pet projects. The pay was OK, not great, but better than most of her friends were getting. Bea spoke American English with no trace of an accent, and when she made deliveries from Rudy's shop, or did PC repairs at people's homes or businesses, usually nobody guessed that she was Brazilian. And, to her deep and private shame, that suited her just fine.

The bus was late. Bea was making up her mind to walk to work, when she heard shouting from the alley behind the laundromat. She walked cautiously over to see what it was. Four young men were brutally beating a small huddled figure, apparently a child, lying on the pavement. One was using a baseball bat, swinging it down at the helpless figure with all his strength. Even from a distance Bea could see the red of the victim's blood staining the bat. A second attacker was attempting to do the same thing with a metal pipe. The other two were kicking the figure, attacking his head, belly and back with heavy boots, while looking around for something else to hit him with. One of the attackers was urging the others on: "Get him! Kill him! He doesn't belong in this world: he is outside the Chain of Being! He's an intruder, the enemy!"

Bea was shocked to recognize this wild-eyed ringleader as Roberto, a close friend of hers from high school. She thought that she knew him well: back then, they had even joked about going to the senior prom together (of course, neither of them had the money for that sort of thing). And he was the quiet, serious sort, the last person she would expect to ever get in trouble or to do anything like… this. Even from this distance, she could see fear and confusion in his eyes, as though he wanted to believe that what he was doing was right, but in his heart he found it repugnant.

Though it seemed like the beating victim was beyond help, Bea felt that she had to do something, just in case. Trying to divert their attention, she called out, "Roberto! E ai, Rapaz? What are you doing?". Roberto looked up, recognized her and answered, "Beatrisa, stay out of this, please!"

Bea had flipped open her cell phone, and pointed it at them. "Stop it now, Roberto! I have the police on the phone and I'm sending them live video of what you're doing!"

This was a bluff (her phone wasn't even turned on), but it worked. The other men dropped their weapons and ran. Roberto called after them, "Where are you going? Don't you remember? Father Oswald told us that we wouldn't get in trouble with the police for killing creatures like this!" But they were gone. Roberto turned to Beatrisa and his voice became very serious. "This so-called 'person' is dangerous. His kind doesn't belong in this world. Father Oswald told us." With that, Roberto was gone.

Bea went over to help the victim: a small man, even shorter than Bea herself. She would have assumed that he was a boy of about 10 or 12 years, except for his face, which was clearly that of an adult. His clothes seemed a little old-fashioned to Bea: he was wearing a short woolen jacket, a cloth cap, and heavy shoes of a style that Bea had never seen before. He was dazed and bleeding, but conscious. "Muito obrigado pela ajuda, thank you so much for helping me" he said. Bea found that bit of token Portuguese annoying, and very puzzling, and ignored it for the moment. "I know one of those boys", she told him. "I can't believe he would do something like this. Can you tell me why they were trying to kill you?"

The small man was silent for a moment. "There is much that I could tell you", he said, "but I need to be certain. About you, I mean. And, by the way, I was not in any real danger there, but I am quite embarrassed to have allowed myself to be seen like that. Under the circumstances, it would have been most convenient for my purposes if they thought they had killed me. But this does in no way diminish your courage and resourcefulness in helping to separate me from those unfortunate misguided souls. And there is also the burden of guilt to consider, should they eventually awaken from this nightmare. Your solution was best, I cannot deny it. I am almost convinced, yes I am almost, in truth."

None of this made the slightest sense to Beatrisa, and she was too shocked to pay much attention to anything but the man's condition. But at this moment he quickly stood up, looking surprisingly unhurt. This little man is tougher than he looks, she thought. "What can I do for you?", she asked. "Can I help you get to the hospital? Or the police station?"

"No thank you, I just need to clean up a bit, I suppose. Some water from the Lower Locks will do just fine, yes, that it will." This was unexpected. He wants to wash up outdoors, in one of the canals? And why would he be so particular about which water he uses? In hopes of getting more information from him, she said, "The Lower Locks? You mean, by the community college?"

The little man was intrigued by this. "Yes, yes. You should go there sometime, you would find O'Malley's class very interesting ..." Then he seemed to focus all of a sudden, and said,

"Beatrisa DeSouza, listen to me! Be very careful! There are dangers all around you, though you do not see them yet! Great and terrible events are coming. You may have a crucial role to play in what is to come. I ask three things of you. First, never cross the river upstream of the Aiken Street Bridge. Second, if you find yourself in trouble that seems impossible to understand and impossible to remedy, seek me out where O'Malley teaches. Third, and most important, stay as far away as you can from Father Oswald. He is an evil man with a wicked and destructive purpose. As your scripture says, by their fruits you shall know them."

With that outburst, he was off at a run, around the corner and gone before Bea could think of how to respond, or what to do next. I guess he's OK, she thought: he gets a beating that should have killed a normal person, and five minutes later he's up and running, as if nothing had happened. That bit about crossing the river was especially strange, though, since her boss at the computer shop had made her promise the same thing when she first took the job.

As she walked on to work, she was most troubled about Roberto. She knew there was no Father Oswald at the local parish, but then again she hadn't seen Roberto at Mass for a long time. Maybe he's joined one of those evangelical churches, she thought. But she had never heard of any church that would demand this sort of behavior.

That's probably the weirdest thing that will happen today, she thought. She hoped.

When she got to the shop, Rudy greeted her with his usual cheerful "Bom dia, Beasuze!". And, as usual, she did not let on how it irritated her when Americans (Jamaican-Americans included) tried to speak Portuguese to her. To him, it was just a habitual friendly gesture, intended to make her feel at home, and that is all it should have meant to her too. Anyway, she still liked her nickname.

The incident on the street continued to prey on her mind throughout the day. Her workload today was relatively dull: mostly replacing power supplies and installing motherboards. So she could not keep herself from brooding. How had he known her name? She had not dwelt on the little man's appearance at the time, but now she was trying to make sense of it. Short and slight of build, he had a face that seemed to be young and old at the same time. Elfin? What do elves look like? Those cartoon guys in the cookie commercials? But those cartoon cookie elves all look exactly like that jackass on the cable news channel... who yammers about illegal aliens 25 hours a day... at ear-splitting volume... on the TV that is always on... at the donut shop... where Mãe works...

Downward spiral. She grabbed a paper towel and wiped the tears off the partially assembled PC that she had been working on. She was glad that Rudy was busy with a customer in the front of the shop. He was a nice guy, and would want to know what was wrong. But explaining would just make things worse. What was wrong was the same thing that was always wrong, the same thing that had always been wrong, and would always be wrong.

****

Rudy Foster was standing behind the checkout counter of his shop, receiving payment from a customer for some PC repairs which Bea had finished yesterday. He noticed that she was upset about something, but guessed that his intrusion would cause more embarrassment than comfort. It wasn't hard to guess the cause of her distress. Being "undocumented" was the very grandmother of troubles, turning even the simplest everyday tasks into nightmarishly impossible trials. And if it wasn't something that had happened to Bea herself, it might be a member of her family, or a friend, or just a member of the community.

Whatever it was that had upset Bea today, Rudy had a strong intuition that it would soon be forgotten in the face of yet more disturbing events. And for him, intuition was not an idle matter: it was the driving force of his life. As a teen in Kingston, he had experienced a vision of unusual power. In fact, he experienced it many times, mostly in dreams but occasionally while he was awake. It was a vision of an evil creature of immense power bent on devouring the entire Earth. A lone warrior was all that stood between the creature and its goal of total destruction. A key character in this vision was a protector, who kept the warrior safe until the time came for the warrior's power and purpose to be revealed. In some instances of the vision the protector failed in his duty, and the result was an Earth as barren of life as its moon. In others, the warrior was prepared in time, defeated the creature, and a glorious new age was born, changing the lives of all human beings for the better in ways that Rudy could vaguely see, but could not clearly comprehend. This was common enough adolescent stuff, but in Rudy's case it was too compelling and persistent to ignore. He had become convinced that he himself was the protector in these visions, and his life's work was finding and preparing this warrior for the task.

This meant that, as soon as he was financially independent, he would leave his family's shop and go north. For many generations, his family had operated an unusual kind of business. In the front of the shop, it was all technology. In the back, it was "equipment and supplies" for real and would-be practitioners of Obeah, Voudon, Santeria, and other traditions of black magic. In the 19th century, the front of the shop had been devoted to eyeglasses, watches and navigational instruments. In the mid-20th century, the emphasis had shifted to radio, and in the present day the front of the Foster shop was devoted to computers, cell phones and other electronics. The Fosters had prospered in both aspects of the business, and now had stores in Mandeville and Spanish Town in addition to the original location in Kingston. There had been a clear progression in the technology part of the business over the years. What was less obvious was the progression in the other part of the business. The Fosters were always happy to sell such things as powdered alligator teeth to fools, but they also kept track of the effectiveness of some of the oils and powders extracted from the leaves and fruits of certain plants, and the roots and bark of certain trees. By refraining from practicing any of the spells or hexes associated with these items, they safeguarded themselves from the harmful consequences of their use. And by keeping track of their customers' practices and experiences, they accumulated a deep knowledge of what actually worked, how it worked, the safest and most effective methods of use, and any consequences to be wary of. "Learn from other people's mistakes, not by making your own" was the unspoken family motto, and made perfect sense for anyone involved in such a potentially dangerous business.

By the time Rudy, now in his thirties, was ready to embark on his quest, he had become an expert in both aspects of the family business. His intuition, which was as clear and compelling as his visions had been, led him inevitably to this cold, rough-edged, eerily quiet city, exhausted yet jittery, a city with troubled spirits stirring aimlessly behind every crumbling wall. Here, he had no difficulty establishing a small computer business. He rented a small storefront in a one-story retail strip on Middlesex Street, on the slope of the hill running down from the Highlands to the Pawtucket Canal. This set of neat white shops was located in the midst of one of Lowell's Cambodian neighborhoods, and Rudy's shop occupied the same block as an Asian food market, a video rental, and a jewelry store. Rudy recognized this location as a sort of nexus, a boundary between the spheres of influence of the Demon and another spirit, benevolent and powerful, which Rudy suspected was the source of his visions. This location put him as close as he dared to the canal and the river. He could see the signs of the Demon's presence, all right: it practically defined the city. And he could see that many others had been vaguely or acutely aware of its presence over the years: how else to explain the

Bowers house, a grand cylindrical bunker built of stone so thick, to protect its inhabitants from… what? And the other rough stone house on Hutchinson Street, much farther from the river, but still clearly built in a hurry, as a refuge from something terrifying, from which only large blocks of stone, and stone of a certain type, would provide protection.

He had no idea whether Obeah or any other such practices had a place in the local culture (and it would have taken decades, at least, to acquire the necessary understanding of whatever forms of conjuring, blessing, cursing and divining might be practiced in the Cambodian community), so he did not attempt to make this a part of his business here. His PC business was an immediate success, and helped him to establish a good network of personal contacts, through which he hoped somehow to find the warrior of his visions, who he knew for certain was in this city. His efforts were rewarded within the year, when the computer lab at the high school, which had been generously endowed and equipped from Rudy's shop, began to be frequented by young Beatrisa. She quickly learned everything about programming that the high school teachers (and their colleagues at the University of Lowell) had to offer, and learned more by studying the raw machine code of the Windows and Mac operating systems (and numerous applications for both). Then, on her own, she took the practice in a strange direction that her teachers had difficulty following. This is how she was brought to Rudy's attention, and despite the fact that he could not rationally work out how expertise, or even brilliance, in computer programming could be used to defeat a terrible world-destroying monster, his intuition told him that she was the one, and there was no point in continuing his search. Either she was the one, or the driving force of his life was meaningless. Bringing her into his business was straightforward. Compared with the alternatives available to the typical young Brazilian, getting this job seemed like a fantastic stroke of luck to Beatrisa.

Though Rudy did not include the other part of his family's traditional business in his current venture, he put to full use everything that his family had learned over the generations. The shop was a fortress of sorts: the most powerful spells of protection and concealment were worked into the doorways, the windows, and all the other vulnerable points of the shop. These spells were so strong that they would stay with Beatrisa even during the hours when she was not at the shop. From the time he had spent in this city, Rudy had become certain that these spells were necessary: that there was someone, human or otherwise, in the city who must be prevented from knowing of Beatrisa's existence.

It was a good arrangement. She was comfortable with the workload, and often found some extremely unusual ways of accomplishing these tasks, being blissfully unaware of what was and wasn't considered acceptable or even possible in the field. Take the customer who just left, for instance. The fool had let his PC's hard drive get so full that defragmenting wouldn't work, and all of its operations had gotten so slow that the box was unusable, but the man had irreplaceable data on this hard drive, and needed help desperately. Bea's approach to this type of task was radical, to put it mildly. Rudy did not try to follow exactly how she went about it, but she thought nothing of rewriting file allocation tables, or creating her own special versions of DOS, Windows, Mac OS, or whatever else might be needed, on the spur of the moment. Apparently, her point of view was: it was all just code, and code could always be modified, or new code written, to do what was needed. After all, that was what computers were for, wasn't it? Things that were unheard-of, and should be impossible, or should take a tremendous amount of time and effort to get right, she seemed to do quickly and flawlessly, always on the first try. Sometimes it even seemed as though she could persuade a computer to find a way to fix itself.

But Bea didn't think she was doing anything special. No one in her family, none of her friends, and almost none of her fellow students back in high school, were especially aware of or interested in computer science. Bea had concluded that it wasn't that important, but it was an easy way to make money and provided her with an opportunity to pursue some interesting projects.

Those "projects"! She had developed an interest in writing programs which had the ability to modify their own code, so that they could evolve according to their "experience" in ways that were not specifically laid out by the programmer. In a sense, they were more like cellular automata than programs in the normal sense, since what they would become over time was difficult to predict, could be fantastically complicated, and the relationship between their initial setup and final evolution was extraordinarily difficult to visualize. The overwhelming majority of self-modifying programs would go inert or self-destruct, either immediately or soon (i.e. within microseconds) after they were launched. However, Bea seemed to have an uncanny knack for preparing self-evolving programs that were not only capable of self-preservation but were in addition benign and actually helpful. They were like living things, motivated by a purpose provided them by Beatrisa. She had read through Wolfram's work on recursive patterns and cellular automata, and had been puzzled by his encyclopedic approach, since in her opinion only the viable, resilient, self-preserving patterns were at all interesting, and it was perfectly obvious (to her) which patterns these were. Although Rudy did not want to ask, he suspected that she had actually used some of these self-evolving programs in her repair work. A hacker unleashing viruses? Perhaps: if so, they were very polite and helpful ones: he had never had any complaints about any of her repairs, and in fact some customers even remarked on how much better their PCs worked, better than when they were brand new.

As clear as his vision was, as obvious and unavoidable as his intuitive decisions had been, Rudy could not feel completely comfortable about the situation. This was the place, there was no doubt. Beatrisa was the warrior, again no doubt. He did not need to look any further: either his adult life had been guided by a delusion, or this was the place where his visions would become real. But was Rudy doing all that he was supposed to do? Was Beatrisa on the path to realizing her purpose and understanding her power (whatever that might be)? Was this casual computer wizardry a part of it, or a distraction? What was worse, he had to keep these worries to himself. He could just imagine her reaction, or that of any sane person, if he explained to her why he was really here in this city, and why he had hired her. She would think him deranged or worse, and run from his protection. He would have failed in his task, and he was all too clearly aware of what that implied. What was not so clear was what else he needed to do in order to succeed. So Rudy Foster waited, watched, and worried.

Chapter 2

In which Charles Healey Stares at some Rocks

(1821 AD)

Charles Healey looked out from the riverbank, at the water rushing over Pawtucket Falls. A mighty noise it made, this tremendous volume of water, over a riverbed whose level dropped by 32 feet in a very short distance. The falls, and their sound, dominated the attention: there were no other sounds or sights in this place to compete with it. On the south side of the river, a few small farms dotted the hillside, separated from one another by chaotic patches of elms and maples. On the north bank, the fading remains of a traditional annual Indian encampment could still be made out, even in the modern year of 1821.

Unlike most waterfalls in Charles' experience, the rocky barrier did not lie directly across the river channel, but made a long diagonal, more parallel than perpendicular. As the river approached from the northwest, it seemed to have every intention of continuing southeastward to Boston, but was quite shocked and surprised to find a series of small hills blocking the way. Charles could easily imagine that the same Power which had placed these hills in the river's way had also opened up the Earth ever so slightly to create the present channel, bending eastward to Newburyport. The water poured over the jagged rocks into this channel, but appeared to do so with reluctance. It continued to rush and bubble with indignation over a further series of rocky drops as the river bent around Ford's Hill.

Charles had been near this place several times in the ten years that he had dwelt in New England, though he preferred to avoid it if he could. But now, with the gentlemen from Boston approaching to survey this very spot, Charles' presence was required, since in fact this was his one and only reason for being in the New World. The gentlemen in question knew about the falls, knew about the 32 foot drop, and when they viewed it with their own eyes, they would most certainly conclude that it was the obvious location for their bold plan: a manufacturing complex for textiles, on a scale never before seen, powered by the water running over these falls: an American industrial establishment to compete directly with the English mills in Lancashire.

Charles saw the falls, knew that the gentlemen were approaching, and understood his task, but the whole situation seemed still so outlandish that he had to know for certain. Ignoring the obvious danger, he scrambled down the bank to where he could see and touch the rocks below the falls. The danger was not the climb itself, though in the November chill there was already ice forming on some of the rocks. Nor was it the danger of the rushing water, since Charles was strong, limber and sure-footed. No, the lurking peril was in the still water above the falls. From his vantage point, that water had taken on an agitated, twitchy, angry look at his approach, as though it wished to bodily rise up over the falls and smash him to bits. He had no doubt that it would if it could. His inspection of the rocks told him that all of the tales had been true, even the most unbelievable ones, and that made his task gravely, terrifyingly important.

As a young man in his native County Cork, Charles Healey had been granted a vision, a heavenly communion, an inspiration of surpassing power and clarity. Some heavenly spirit, radiant with the Grace of God, had revealed to him that a Demon from the depths of Hell, imprisoned somewhere in the wilds of the New World, was endeavoring to break free. This was a creature of such awful power and malice that its release would bring on an Apocalypse, not the Second Coming as described in Revelations, but a premature and abrupt Apocalypse, something that served only Satan's purposes. But his vision also revealed that it was within the power of mortals like himself to thwart this plan, and to make certain that this horrible creature could no longer threaten Creation.

Young master Healey awoke from this vision filled with the determination to fulfill his role in this battle, but with no idea of precisely what he could do. Fortunately, the beneficiaries of such special grace as Charles had experienced often take on a special aura that can be perceived by others who possess the necessary sensitivity and knowledge. Monsignor Fenwick, of Charles' parish, noticed the change in Charles at the very next Mass, and took him aside later that day to educate Charles in the broader implications of his experience.

At first this education was rather shocking and disturbing. Charles had assumed that the source of his inspiration must be a saint or an angel, though It had never actually identified Itself. However, rather than sort this out for him, the Monsignor gave Charles a book about Greek mythology and asked him to read it through. This did not take Charles very long to do, and afterwards Fenwick told him that the Greeks were very close to the truth, that there were beings in the world which were like the Titans and the Gods of their stories. But Fenwick insisted on referring to these Titans as "Firsts" and the Gods as "Seconds" (as though they were courses of a meal, Charles thought). The Firsts were unimaginably old, many hundreds of millions of years in fact, and they were Earth's first form of life. Their physical substance consisted of complex patterns of circulation of the air, of the water, and of molten rock beneath the ground. Long before the first worm, insect, blade of grass or slimy bit of algae made its appearance, the Firsts had attained a deep and subtle intelligence, and a community of harmonious cooperation, making the world a nursery for life of the more familiar kind. Intelligence they had (and have) in abundance, but their thought processes are commensurate with their lifespans: operating with glacial slowness, so that the only aspect of it that a human could hope to apprehend in one lifetime was a frozen instant of thought, in all its static detail much like the instructions sent by a master chess player playing a game by mail, if in one mailing he not only specified his next move, but also included responses to every possible countermove, for many moves in advance.

The Seconds were a different matter. By contrast, they had only been in existence a relatively short time, only ten thousand years (and Charles was pretty sure that even this predated Genesis by a goodly amount, which troubled him deeply). According to the Monsignor, the Seconds were beings like the Firsts: similar in substance, though without the full depth of understanding, but much quicker in their actions and thoughts. They were created in response to the development of agriculture by human beings. With this new mode of human sustenance, the movements and actions of humans no longer followed the patterns established by wind and water, but took on arbitrary shapes and forms. Some of these the Firsts found intolerably destructive of the careful balance they had established: in much the same way that a soprano's high note can shatter glass. The Seconds had the ability to speak directly to humans in their minds, to lead them away from practices hurtful to the Firsts, and toward different practices that were beneficial to all, though the humans might not be capable of understanding why this was so.

To a soul raised in the comfort of the simple certainties of the One True Church, all of this went far beyond heresy: it went beyond madness, even. Charles was a serious-minded youth, and approached these issues with gravity. But he had the evidence of his senses to consider. And Monsignor Fenwick was a man of the Church, highly regarded by his peers and his flock alike, and he had a way of making all of this dangerous lunacy seem reasonable, even obvious. When Charles raised the objection that all of what he had been told was in direct contradiction to what he had read in the Old Testament, and had learned in Catechism, Fenwick had cautioned him not to form hasty judgments until he had acquired a great deal more experience in life, particularly judgments regarding what did and did not constitute a contradiction. He promised Charles that one day he would attain the wisdom to reconcile the truth of the world with the truth of Scripture. For his part, Charles resolved to do his best to acquire that wisdom, because this conflict made for a deep and nagging discomfort in his soul.

All of this information which Monsignor Fenwick had conveyed to young Charles Healey must have been hard-won, since it appeared that the Seconds used their gift of communication sparingly, and endeavored, when possible, to speak only to those who would not be driven mad by the experience. Fenwick had somehow made coherent sense of a great accumulation of inconsistent and highly dubious tales. If he had been blessed by such contact himself, he did not see fit to mention it, and Charles thought it would be rude to inquire. Perhaps the Monsignor had not worked alone in the acquisition and preservation of this knowledge. Again, Charles had no way of knowing, and the Monsignor did not volunteer this information.

There was one other persistent theme in these tales, a reason for Monsignor Fenwick to react with alarm at the substance of Charles' information. In the background of the various communications between Seconds and humans over the centuries, there was a recurring rumor of an Evil One imprisoned in a faraway place, a Demon whose release would spell doom entire and final for the world of the living. In Fenwick's view, Charles' vision, focused specifically on this danger, gave in its details a time and place to the threat. The place was the new nation of the United States of America, and the time was now, or at least very soon. From various details of Charles' vision (a camp of praying Indians, an immense fist made of water, a prison door made of stone), Fenwick was able to surmise that the place in question was a certain town in Massachusetts, along the Merrimack River.

So, with his legs aching from the rush of the icy cold water, Charles, older and in some ways wiser, finally had to accept the truth of yet another of the Monsignor's wild claims. The story was that, in order to imprison the Evil One, the Firsts had split a small continent in two, and had flung the western part against North America, while the eastern part drifted the opposite way and eventually became the foundation for Ireland, Portugal, and even a part of cursed England (may it be transported whole straight to Hell). This had been done because there was something in this rock with which the Demon could not abide contact. In this place, this Pawtucket Falls on the Merrimack River in Massachusetts, a Demon, whose substance animated the water of the river, was held at bay behind the rocks over which the water tumbled noisily, though the Demon itself could not pass. The rocks were a barrier between the Demon and the open sea some miles downstream, the sea which would give the Demon an overwhelming power to match its pent-up fury, the power to achieve its aim of universal destruction, should it find a way to reach it.

A Demon with a lifespan measured in hundreds of millions of years had a variety of options available. The natural processes of erosion would ultimately wear away any rock, and cover it with silt, and make it possible for the Demon to pass. But this would take many lifetimes, and thus could not be the crisis that Charles was called upon to address. In fact, the Monsignor had told him that the Merrimack itself had once flowed on a different course, meeting the Atlantic in Boston Harbor rather than Newburyport, and that the outcroppings of "Irish Rock" had indeed worn down and been silted over through the long ages. However, as evidence of the Firsts' far-reaching perspicacity, an Ice Age had been brought about before the Demon could consummate its escape in this manner, the mile-thick ice sheet immobilizing the Demon and its water for a time. At the end of this Ice Age, the retreating ice had dropped some of its burden of rock and soil in precisely such a way as to divert the Merrimack to its present course, flowing directly over this very outcropping. Charles suspected that the hill over which he had walked to this place from Frye's Tavern (along a cowpath that would in the very near future be named School

Street) was one such heap, and the other hills in the vicinity were of like kind. Charles had also felt occasional small earthquakes in this area, and he knew that this usually meant that the ground in some places was rising by very small degrees, and the ground in other places was not. He guessed that this was part of the plan as well, to keep the bare imprisoning "Irish" rock exposed faster than the forces of erosion could cover it.

Of course, the arrival of humans, and especially Europeans, on the scene changed the balance completely. The evidence was within sight, just upstream from the falls: the entrance to the Pawtucket Canal. This canal, built in 1794 for the purpose of transporting logs around the falls to the shipyards at Newburyport (at least that is why people thought they were building it), was suspiciously easy to lay out: there was a sluggish stream emptying into the Merrimack, another sluggish stream emptying into the Concord River, and a shallow marsh in between. The canal's opening ceremonies had been marked by a bizarre incident, of which Charles had heard varying accounts. A barge, loaded up with dignitaries from the surrounding towns and from Boston, was set in motion from the canal mouth toward the first set of locks. It had not even gotten clear of the river when (according to some sources), a pair of huge hands composed entirely of water rose up and gripped the sides of the barge, partially crushing it and dragging it abruptly to the bottom of the shallow water. Several people died in the attack, although this fact was kept out of the official records. Others were driven mad, and lived out their days shrieking about what they had seen in the water in that instant, to anyone who would listen, or to no one at all.

Notwithstanding its macabre debut, the Pawtucket Canal was well used for its intended purpose: that is, until a competing canal was completed, running from a point just a mile or so upstream of the falls, all the way to Boston Harbor. The Middlesex Canal, ironically laid out along the original ancient course of the Merrimack, diverted the flow of precious raw materials to Boston, ultimately eclipsing Newburyport as a shipbuilding center.

Charles counted himself (and the world) fortunate in that the Middlesex Canal could never provide an escape route for the Demon. It was too narrow, too long, and the locks were lined with too much of that stone which the Demon could not approach. And most important, it flowed the wrong way: its waters flowed both north and south from a high point in Billerica. He could count himself lucky in one other respect as well. The Pawtucket Canal, which was clearly the escape route that the Demon desired, also contained too much of that same stone in its locks and linings. This told Charles that, while the canal itself might have been built in response to its incessant psychic demands, the creature did not have any human confederates involved in its construction (at least, none that were both sane and healthy). But it was not safe to assume that this would always be so.

On this day the Pawtucket Canal lay moribund, in disrepair, but presenting no immediate danger. But it was about to be brought back to life, broadened and ramified, at the hands of some industrial visionaries. If this was not done with the necessary safeguards…

He had seen enough. The gentlemen would be there at any moment, and if they saw him there at the Falls, it would complicate his task. He had come up here from Boston a day ahead of these other gentleman, and stationed himself at Frye's Tavern, near the Swamp Locks, where anyone traveling by stage would be certain to stop for refreshment. His purpose was to make sure that when he introduced himself and his proposal to them, there would be a plausible reason for him to be aware of their plans, from supposedly having overheard their conversations. Of course, he had learned much more from his network of spies, both in Boston and Waltham. If the worthies of the Boston Associates found the site to their liking (as they most surely would), they would refurbish the old Pawtucket Canal, and dig a network of new canals within its arc to supply motive power for a cluster of textile mills on an unprecedented scale. He, Charles Healey, had to quietly take control of this effort to insure that it was done safely, and all the while he had to watch for evil or deluded men who might be helping the Demon in some way.

Charles would propose to the industrialists that they should accomplish their purpose most swiftly by employing crews of itinerant Irish laborers, which crews he, Mr. Charles Healey, could personally produce. And, since Charles was capable of moderating his speech and mannerisms to appear a little less "Irish" and a little more "English" (though it did make him want to throttle himself at times), these men of business would feel comfortable enough dealing with him that they might be able to overcome their ignorant revulsion at the people who would be doing their dirty work. It was an excellent proposal. Charles knew that he could deliver, and he also knew that as long as he believed in it sufficiently himself, he could make these cursed greedy arrogant uncouth Yankee swine believe as well.

Edging carefully downstream, keeping out of sight of the men approaching from the south, Charles left the riverbank at the edge of the Fletcher farm, and made his way along a dusty cart path that would a few short years hence be named Merrimack Street, and headed up a small hill (which would, in those same few short years, become known as Chapel Hill), by way of another cart path whose name would be Gorham Street. On the other side, he paused by Hale's mill, a modest affair (by the standards of what was to come) powered by a small brook, which chose this spot to pour its blessed happy waters into the Concord River, well away from the brook's origins in the woodlands of Chelmsford and Carlisle. Charles always found himself cheered and comforted in the presence of this brook, and believed that it contained the essence of the spirit which had sent him on this journey so many years ago. From Hale's mill he circled back to Frye's Tavern and settled himself at a table in the corner, nursing a tankard of ale until the gentlemen returned. As he waited, he tried to sort out his opinions regarding the men he would be dealing with, and the sleepy Yankee farming community which would be obliterated by their efforts, as surely as those farmers' immediate forebears had obliterated all signs of the community of Christian "Praying Indians" which had existed here.

In Ireland, young Charles had not had so much as two farthings to rub together, let alone enough for the Atlantic crossing. But Monsignor Fenwick had stepped in, using Church funds to pay his passage. But not being one to waste Church money, Fenwick had insisted that Charles disembark at Halifax, to avoid the entry fees for the Irish at American ports. So Charles had dutifully complied, and took the "stroll" across the border and south to Massachusetts. Along the way, he found the woodland paths of Maine and New Hampshire already well-trodden with Irish feet. The plain fact was that he, and a goodly percentage of his countrymen, dwelt in the United States illegally. But in this young nation, with more work to be done than there were able hands to do it, enforcement was lax or nonexistent. It mattered not to the New Englanders: the Yankee farmers looked down their inbred noses on all Irish equally, scorning the ones who arrived legally as much as the ones who did not. Of course, it was Charles' view that if these self-satisfied folks, who considered the Irish such a scourge, had applied themselves with a bit more vigor, both in their fields and in their bedchambers, there would have been no incentive for the Irish to come here in the first place. Charles had no love for the industrialists from Boston, but by the same token had no sympathy whatever for the locals who were about to be victimized by them. At any rate, the task at hand was of much greater importance than the self-interest of any such group, small or large.

Finally the men from the Boston Associates made their appearance, their inspection complete. They were all there, the movers and shakers in this unusual enterprise. There was Nathan Appleton, the dapper financier; Paul Moody, the sober and brooding mechanical engineer; and Patrick Tracy Jackson, who currently managed the pilot factory in Waltham. And there as well was young Kirk Boott, a former British Army officer, a creature of consuming arrogance and ambition, who saw this new venture as a way to establish his rightful position in the world. Charles expected that Boott was the one whom he would have to persuade, and then deal with on an ongoing basis, and knew that he would earn his place in Heaven by enduring this fate.

Conspicuously absent from the group, having died just a scant four years ago, was the man who had made their project possible: Francis Cabot Lowell, the Moses of the American textile industry, the man who had led his people to the Promised Land but who, like the Moses of the Israelites, was not permitted to enter the land himself. Lowell had singlehandedly made possible large-scale manufacturing in the United States by means of a bold act of industrial espionage, one that would probably never be equaled in its impact. On a tour of the mills of Lancaster, Lowell, like all other visitors, had been forbidden to carry paper and pencil, forbidden to make notes on what he saw. But Francis Cabot Lowell nonetheless committed to memory the essentials of the power looms' mechanical designs, and on his return recreated and improved upon them in his laboratory in Boston, and then in a small facility in Waltham, using the Charles River as motive power. This river had proven inadequate to power a truly large-scale establishment, one that would compete directly with English mills. And so, the search for a mightier source of power had led his disciples to the banks of the Merrimack. To a waterfall that already had a serious purpose beyond their reckoning.

They sat down at a large table, ordered a meal, and spread out some papers with hastily sketched maps and designs for machinery, which became the focus of some excited discussion. This was the opportunity that Charles needed.

"Humbly begging your pardon, Sirs", he said as he strode up to their table, "I must confess that I could not help listening to your conversation, and find it most intriguing" Although by his clothing, his speech and his bearing, Charles made no secret of being Irish, he somehow managed to appear not at all exotic, and to these New Englanders appeared reassuringly sober, articulate and confident. Still they were skeptical. Kirk Boott responded to this overture in a predictably patronizing tone. "You are correct, young fellow, it is indeed intriguing. We plan to harness the power of yonder river, in the service of striking a mortal blow at British industry. Although I would hardly expect you to understand how that will be done". Boott then went silent and they all waited for this Irish fellow to amuse them with his incomprehension.

To the great surprise of all, instead of being visibly bewildered by the mental picture of a river with a harness strapped across it, he responded, "I can see why you are interested in this location. What you require is a large flow of water dropping by a considerable height, and a means of diverting that water to drop in the place of your choosing. Here you have the mighty Pawtucket Falls to provide the power, and with the Pawtucket Canal, though it may have fallen into disuse, you have your delivery system already nearly half built."

Since it would have been understandable for these gentlemen to pass swiftly from mean-spirited condescension directly to hostile suspicion, Charles quickly attempted to place the astuteness of his observation in a harmless context. "Meaning no harm, Sirs, I have considerable experience in the building and maintenance of canals, which is why, as I stated, your conversation was so intriguing to me, and why I listened so keenly".

Before the opportunity, now so tentatively opened up, could evaporate, he quickly made his case. "Your plans strike me as most ambitious, as the canal in question is in poor condition, and must be refurbished to begin with, by those who understand this type of work. Other difficulties concerning rocks and soil will present themselves as you begin to extend branches from this canal toward your mill sites, and may give you some concern regarding the exact locations of branch canals and mills. You will need many hands to accomplish the initial construction. This can be quite costly in itself, and the involvement of those hands in your enterprise, unless chosen and watched carefully, may bring in other areas of unforeseen risk which may be as costly as any of the aspects of the project which you have accounted for. Remember, you have a community of suspicious churchgoing farmers whose approval you will require as you begin the tearing asunder of a good part of their lands and turning them into something new and strange"

This brought the response he was seeking from Kirk Boott: "Am I to understand that you believe you have something to offer us in the pursuance of this project?"

"That is exactly what you are to understand, good Sir", replied Charles. "I have at my disposal a worthy crew of strong Irish workmen, who will work for lower wages than the Yankee folk, yet are utterly reliable, and will work under my expert direction and unsparing eye. Should you choose to avail yourself of our services, I can have this disciplined crew in this place as quickly as two days after the ink is dry on the contract. We will dig your canals, we will build your locks, they will be built to last, and they will deliver the motive power that you require for your mills. Which we will also build!"

It was actually easier than he had anticipated. They were eager to do business. Perhaps they had already recognized the necessity of cheap Irish labor, and quailed at the difficulties of hiring and managing such workers, with their reputation for idling, drunkenness, theft and violence. Charles presented such a convincing picture of an orderly group of laborers, and of his own expertise in supervising the construction work, that their understandable fears had been completely assuaged.

There were some minor flaws in his proposal, however. For one thing, Charles Healey had no such "crew at his disposal". That was an outright lie. He also had no experience in canal building. Fortunately, there were three things that Charles did have which would counterbalance these lacks. One was an unshakable and well-founded confidence in his ability to improvise. Another was a deep insight as to how any kind of mechanical work could be done, regardless of whether he had ever seen work of this kind before. And his third asset was that he was on first name terms with every tavern keeper in Charlestown. The proper word, and the proper coin, dropped in these establishments would rapidly provide him with an army of Irish muscle, ready and willing to take on any task, be it wholesome or otherwise.

Monsignor Fenwick had recently written to Charles, on the subject of this latest development. He told Charles that, in view of the dangerous and unpredictable nature of the situation, he was preparing to recruit a Third to make the passage, to come and help. The very thought of this gave Charles the shivers: here was yet another kind of living being not mentioned in the Good Book, and mentioned only sporadically and inconsistently in Greek legends, Thirds, known by another name, were all too familiar in Irish folktales, and were never known to bring good fortune to those who sought their help. While he was obliged to accept that the Monsignor knew best, he fervently hoped and prayed that Fenwick would change his mind about sending a Third. And he wondered at the unsavory company that the Monsignor must be keeping, for a man of the Church, to be able to bring such a thing about.

As for Charles, he would need one more thing to insure the success of his task as he understood it. He needed to obtain some more of that good Irish rock, from Ireland. An odd thing to call for, perhaps, but this rock could be shipped unobtrusively as ships' ballast, beneath the notice of suspicious eyes. Charles felt that it was worth the extra effort and expense. No point in leaving things to chance. Keeping the world safe from unimaginably ancient demons is not a task to be carried out in a half-arsed manner, no indeed it is not.

Chapter 3

In which the Creature does Harm

The afternoon light was fading quickly as Frank Diorio pulled onto the highway along the river, on his way home from the office. The Planning Board meeting this afternoon had been frustrating and confusing. As an attorney for Thomson Development, his job was simply to present his client's plans for the Western Avenue Towers project. It was such an obvious boon to a blighted area of the city that Board approval should have been a mere formality. As it turned out, the Board turned him down flat before he had gotten halfway through his presentation. It must have been that smug bastard Wilkins. The man had hardly spoken during the session, just favored him with a nasty smirk the whole time. Most of the Board members seemed terrified of him, but why? Thomson Development had negotiated agreements with all of the sellers, had the architectural plans completed by one of the most prestigious firms in Boston, and the project had enthusiastic support from many civic organizations in Lowell. But even Jones, Bradford and Eang, board members who had previously assured Frank of their support, voted against him. What was going on?

Frank had grown up in Lowell, and had a strong desire to see this development happen. He had personally witnessed how the city had been brought back to life by the restoration of the old mill buildings, a grand concept first championed by Patrick Mogan and then taken up in a big way by the National Park Service. Refurbishing abandoned mill buildings and turning them to new uses while preserving their historical character was a new idea in the 70s, and its spectacular success in Lowell had led in time to similar projects in other cities in New England and around the world. The textile industry which had made Lowell an important city in the 19th century had abandoned it in the early 20th. As a result of changes in technology, demographics and economics, Lowell gradually ceased to be a profitable location for this type of manufacturing. It came to the point where the city was crowded with abandoned mill buildings, which neither the owners nor the city had the money or the will to tear down. Now, transformed, some had become the headquarters of the Lowell National

Historical Park; many others now housed apartments and offices. And every year in July, the revitalization project was displayed in its full glory as the world flocked to Lowell for the annual Folk Festival, a showcase for musical talent from all over the world.

Frank had been a child when all this began, and its impact was a part of his life. Lately, his attention had turned increasingly to another area of the city, as "dead" as the mills had once seemed. There was a span of land lying along the old Pawtucket Canal which seemed to resist all efforts at development, and was filled with storage lots for old buses and trucks, half-started businesses, and large stretches of weed-choked vacant lots. In view of what had been accomplished in the city during his lifetime, this seemed ridiculous to Frank. This was the geographical heart of the city. It was as if all of the other four boroughs of New York City had been built up, and it had never occurred to anyone to build anything on Manhattan Island. It was a swath of very cheap land, currently a well-known playground for addicts and violent gangs in the evening (and sometimes during the day as well), but it could be so much more, and Frank was not the only one who believed this.

He would meet with the client tomorrow to try and sort out a new strategy. For now, he just needed to get home, have a nice meal, and try and relax with Jean and the kids and put the unpleasant business behind him for the evening. But this headache wouldn't go away. The view of the river from the road, which should have been soothing, only disturbed him more. It seemed grey, agitated, threatening.

As the road made a turn he saw something standing in the lane ahead that he couldn't believe. From far away it looked like a dead tree, but fleshy and slimy, with "branches" waving around. As he got closer, he saw that the "branches" were actually long sinuous necks, each with a dragon head. He recognized what this apparition was: a creature out of Greek mythology, a Hydra. How could such a thing exist, and how could be occupying the middle of the lane on the VFW Highway? To make things worse, in spite of the gathering darkness of late afternoon, it seemed illuminated by a strange light that came from nowhere: a sickly glow of yellow, pink and green. This did not make sense, and he found the sight of it profoundly depressing. Either his mind was diseased, or there was something in the world which truly had no right to exist.

It sure looked real, though. And when those dragon mouths opened, their shrieks seemed to come from inside his head. All these observations had registered in less than a second, and Frank lost no time swerving around the impossible creature. Horns blared from cars in the other lane. None of the other drivers seemed to even notice the creature. How could that be?

Without giving him any time to recover, a second Hydra appeared before him in the left lane. This one was also unnaturally illuminated, and was also shrieking at him. He swerved into the right lane to avoid it, narrowly escaping a collision with a car in that lane. A few seconds later, another Hydra, larger than before, appeared on the road in the right lane. On this Hydra, in place of two of the dragon heads were human heads, although larger than normal. Frank did a double take, because these were the heads of his mother and father, who had died only last year. Like the dragon heads, they were yelling, but now he could make it out as, "Let me out! Let me out Dammit!" Again, it seemed to Frank that he was the only one who was seeing these things.

Head throbbing, with panic taking hold, Frank swerved left onto the median, only to see yet another Hydra in his path, this time with heads of his wife and children, but still shrieking in the same psychotic voice: “Let me out!” In his panic, Frank had not mustered the presence of mind to slow down at all, and was having great difficulty maintaining control as his Taurus bumped along the median strip at 60 MPH. He lost control utterly as yet another Hydra appeared, this time with heads that all had his own face, still recognizable though distorted with berserk rage. Some of these heads detached themselves from the Hydra body and flew directly at his windshield.

Frank was by this point unable to see, and frozen with terror. He was doomed already. But, to make things worse, all of a sudden his steering wheel became red-hot and his foot on the accelerator became too heavy to lift. Hardly even noticing this, Frank swerved off the opposite side of the median and into oncoming traffic. Within seconds, he and his car were totally demolished by a heating oil delivery truck.

****

At City Hall, still in his office, "Sam Wilkins" did not hear the crash, though he did hear the sirens of the fire engines and ambulance rushing to the scene, and he knew that this little task was accomplished. It had been a good idea to direct the Master's attention onto this one, he thought. Its form of "communication", these images that It placed in people's minds, were usually fatal to humans, or at least caused permanent damage. It took a huge effort of concentration on Wilkins' part to help the Master to identify an individual human. However, knowing that the victim would be in close proximity to the river made things much easier. The effort was worthwhile, because this one had been the driving force for development in the Passageway, which Wilkins had labored for more than a century to keep clear of obstacles to the Master's escape.

Of course, Wilkins himself was damaged: too damaged in fact to understand how damaged he was. His earliest memory was of waking up in the year 1835. He knew himself to be named Moss, and knew that he had gone by the name Musgo (in the Spanish colonies, presumably). He even knew that he had once gone by the name Ikech, although he did not remember that this had been the very same name in an obscure, long-lost dialect of a people who had been absorbed into the Incan empire. For he was quite old: he had been born (if that is the right term) in 1507, and early in his life had traveled north from the Andes mountains in response to the spread of agricultural technology in North America, and rumors of the appearance of European explorers on the Atlantic coast. His duties were typical of Thirds: carrying out necessary tasks in the physical realm that the Seconds could not persuade humans to do through dreams and visions, or which humans would not be capable of, no matter how well motivated.

Shortly after his arrival in the Massachusetts colony, in the year 1708, he had been stricken by the creature in the river. This was a terrible stroke of bad luck: the creature had been flailing about wildly with its psychic onslaughts, hoping to strike the emperor Passaconaway, who at this time was no longer reachable. Recognizing a fleshly mortal of similar abilities, It unleashed all its destructive power on this Third. The result was a sort of coma lasting more than a century, in which Moss had wandered about, alive but mindless. He finally woke up, in the Master's power, in 1835, in a world which he barely recognized, though he would have been hard-pressed to explain what kind of world he should have recognized. The bad luck for the world was that now the thing in the river had an awesomely effective servant, with the physical and mental capabilities of a Third, and what was much worse, the same ferocious dedication to his purpose.

Moss had taken on various names and identities in the years since then, always placing himself in a position where he could control most of what went on in the canal system and the areas nearby, without being overly conspicuous. Many years were devoted to undoing the safeguards put in place by that meddler Healey. Moss had also worked diligently to insure that the Passageway remained mostly vacant, undeveloped, and unnoticed. As he had learned over the years, it wasn't necessary to kill everyone who might want to cause trouble by starting major building projects there, as long as enough bad things happened to create an atmosphere of vague unease, which would make people turn away from such plans without necessarily knowing why.

Working on behalf of the Master had its rewards. He enjoyed the power he held over short-lived humans, enjoyed manipulating them and seeing them react in their predictable ways. There were drawbacks as well. The Master was not easy to please, and was capable of inflicting excruciating, soul-shaking pain without warning or explanation. Sometimes it seemed like a punishment, but other times it made no sense at all. The other drawback was… Wilkins' train of thought stopped short as he realized that he couldn't remember what the "other drawback" might have been. And worst of all, any time he tried to remember such things, or remember exactly when and how he was recruited into the Master's service, he got such a terrible headache that he had to discipline himself to avoid these subjects. Despite his skill and long success in controlling the weak humans, he himself felt confused and off balance most of the time. This was easy enough to conceal from the foolish humans he lived and worked among, though, just as it was easy to conceal his true nature from them.

There was a light tap on his office door. It was the crew from Silva Cleaners, making their nightly rounds through the building. They knew he often worked late, so it made sense to knock. He had certainly made life unpleasant at times for janitorial workers who came in without knocking, or even those that did knock, if he was in a nasty mood. And there was that one occasion when one of those guys had lost his temper and taken a swing at him in response to a particularly harsh and gratuitous spate of abuse.

Wilkins may have looked like someone who could be physically intimidated, but that guy sure had a surprise in store for him. With the hex that Wilkins slapped on him, he could never find his way out of the building again, and no other human person would be able to see or hear him. The guy must have starved to death by now, Wilkins thought. Probably a good idea to get that disposed of. Even dead bodies that no one can see are sort of unhealthy to have around. Talk about your "sick building syndrome"!

Wilkins had already caused enough pain and death for today, so he just gathered up his briefcase and grumpily left his office. If the office cleaners had watched him proceed down the hallway, they might have noticed that he suddenly vanished from view about halfway to the stairs. Most of them were strongly disinclined to watch, however. It was bad enough that they had to come up to this floor in the first place, and even worse that "O Monstrinho" was still there at this hour.

A mile or so upriver, beneath the water surface, It brooded. Its thoughts, if they could be interpreted in terms of human modes of thought, were a static mass of impatience, anxiety, resentment, hostility and psychotic fury, broadcasting to any living being within several thousand miles, "Let me out!! Clear a path for me!!" Over time, trillions of insects, billions of birds and millions of small mammals had mindlessly responded, moving a spec of dirt here, a grain of sand there, or a small pebble or twig. Of course, often the command backfired, as the Passageway would be clogged with the corpses of insects, birds or mammals who were overwhelmed by the psychic onslaught. The net result over time, *following the retreat of the last glacial ice sheet, had been the formation of one small creek bed running into the Merrimack River just upstream of the Falls, another running into the Concord River close to its end at the Merrimack, and, nearly connecting the two, a small swampy area. When the land of East Chelmsford was set aside for the "praying Indians" under the tutelage of John Eliot, this was clearly the result of some maneuvering by that troublesome Passaconaway, to protect the Passageway for as long as possible. At the end of the 18th century, with the "Indians" long gone and the land taken over again by the Chelmsford farmers, the relentless psychic pressure of the Demon's demands led to further excavation of this channel, now being called the Pawtucket Canal. This was not yet the escape route that It needed, since the path was broken up by a series of locks, but it was a step in the right direction, and a being with a billion-year lifespan could confidently count on structures to crumble over time. All in all, it had been a good idea to lure people from Europe to this continent with seductive promises of riches and moral conquest, because these Europeans were very much in the habit of digging canals. And now, they had explosives as well.*

LET ME OUT!!!!

Chapter 4

In which the Professor gets it Wrong, and Tin gets Further Instructions

The March chill drifted into the lecture hall along with the students. It was midafternoon, and the sky outside was grey, as was the mood in the hall. They were here for the first lecture in a special series, “Mythology and Perception”, taught by Professor Ron O’Malley. If any of the students thought it was odd that this course should be offered by the Anthropology department instead of Humanities, nobody was complaining. As one student muttered to his friend, "As long as it fulfils the science requirement, that's fine with me." His companion replied, "I hear this guy is famous or something. He was offered a professorship at Harvard but turned it down to teach here."

"What is he, nuts?" That question seemed to arise with regularity regarding this particular professor. After some brief formalities, Professor O'Malley launched into his introduction:

"I would like to begin this course by pointing out that each one of you labors under a pervasive delusion. This delusion is what makes it possible for you to function during your waking hours.

"That delusion is your quaint notion that the world that you experience with your senses is identical to some objective reality. I do not mean that you are experiencing a delusion or a dream. Let me assure you, the situation is far worse than that. In fact, we are all physiologically incapable of 'perceiving' reality as we pretend to understand the term."

At this point, several students hurriedly checked their schedules to make sure they had not wandered into a philosophy course by mistake. But there it was, Anthropology 305, taught by Ronald O'Malley.

He continued: "The problem is that our species is at an intermediate state of evolution. Our brains are extremely good at absorbing and processing sensory data, but their ability to analyze and digest this information, to transform it into an accurate model of the world, is not at the same level. So we spend a good part of our childhood learning how to reject, exclude or ignore most of what impinges on our senses, and constructing conceptual boxes in which to tuck away most of what's left, so that there is very little immediate experience left for us to actually contend with. If our bodies are vehicles, our minds reside in cockpits with movie screens instead of windows, displaying scenes that we project from within, and blocking most of the information from outside.

"We live in an anxious age that is intolerant of uncertainty. Science has made such impressive strides in understanding so much of what happens in the world that we complacently believe that everything that might ever happen in our experience is logically explainable based on principles that are already understood. You would no doubt find it very comical to hear someone making this assumption, say, 500, or even 100, years ago.

"Even the things that are not understood have boundaries drawn around them and labels affixed, to give the illusion of understanding. Nonlinear processes? Phenomena happening on the Earth's surface that are not described by any equations yet developed? One example of such phenomena is the weather! Would you call this a trivial exception, or something important? What if the nonlinear processes occurring all around us were the actions of living entities? Of consciousness? What if they were the living entities themselves?"

This brought an audible gasp from the back of the lecture hall. When some students turned to look, however, they found themselves somehow unable to focus clearly on whoever it was who made the sound.

O'Malley continued on the theme of his lecture: "In most traditions of mythology and folklore you will find the notion that the currents of nature are animated by conscious beings, whether they are called gods, spirits, or whatever. I find this at least as sensible as calling them 'nonlinear processes' and pretending they can be dismissed by applying a label. The point is that an attempt to perceive and understand reality should make full use of all possible concepts and modes of thinking.

"If it sounds like I am devaluing the accomplishments of science, that is unfortunate and is not my intention. Mainly, I am criticizing the intellectual complacency that has become commonplace in modern life, using the accomplishments of science as an excuse for avoiding critical thought.

"Our religions also feed our complacency on the spiritual side. They thrill us with the vision that gods once danced upon the earth, but comfort us with the assurance that they are now kept at a safe distance. Instead of teaching us how to perceive miracles occurring in our midst, they supply us with reasons why miracles should not happen!"

Drawing himself up with a long breath, O'Malley continued to his conclusion:

"Enough of my complaints. I wish to explain what this course is about. Together we will attempt to explore the breadth of ways, and modes of perception, in which our fellow humans have experienced existence. This must be done without prejudice. It must also be done without becoming enmeshed or infatuated with the pleasantly exotic. Mythology and folklore provide the richest source for this exploration, and we will be taking a very serious look at what the different stories that come down to us might actually mean. Keep in mind also that more humans exist now on the earth than ever before, so some of the answers we seek may be freshly created next door, or somewhere halfway around the world, as we speak.

"The best way I can express the ultimate goal of this study is by analogy. Take a look at the screen." On the screen above him, O'Malley had projected a slide which showed three different data plots:

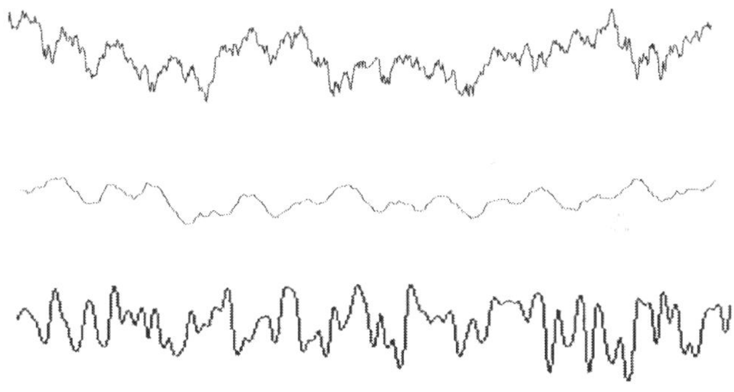

"One of these plots shows the value of the Dow Jones Industrial Average over a period of four months. One of them shows the daily barometric pressure in Chicago over the past five years. And one of them is the digitized sound file of a few seconds of Beethoven's Ninth Symphony. They all look a bit similar, don't they? Similar in their apparent randomness and lack of discernible meaning. Yet we have the capability of perceiving one of these data streams in such a way that we can discern the separate melodic lines of violins, trumpets, horns, and several different human voices. Is there anything about any of these three plots that would suggest it contains such profound meaning that every one of us is capable of perceiving? Of course not! You can't tell by looking at the data this way.

"So much of the sensory experience that the world presents us with is like that seemingly incomprehensible data stream. It signifies nothing to us, and we reject it because its apparent lack of meaning is offensive and annoying. But my question, my eternal question, the only question is: what is the music that surrounds us, that we are unable to hear? A critical but open-minded study of modes of perception in human cultures through the ages may help us answer that question.

"Next week we will get down to cases, starting with the Sumerians. Your recommended reading is listed in the handouts. I wish you all a good week."

As the students gathered up their books and began to exit the lecture hall, many were seriously considering whether or not to drop this course. Some also exchanged some rather unkind speculation as to the professor's sanity.

The student in the back row, with the oddly old-fashioned clothes and pointed ears, did not look amused by all this. His name was Tin, and those ears would have identified him as a Third, had anyone been capable of seeing them. But with his concealment spell in place, he simply stood up and followed the line of students out of the lecture hall. At the door he stole a last lingering look at this Professor O'Malley, and raised an eyebrow. The man was so close, and yet...-Mo Dia- how badly the figure by the door wanted to unleash the true light of it all on him. This one was definitely one of those whom the Bashaba and Wamesit had sent him here to find, along with the girl from Brazil, and that other one, who kept eluding his grasp. If these people were to help, they had to know the truth, all that was hidden and more besides. But Tin must wait. He had located two of these people, and now he must return, report and discuss what to do next.

Quickly, he ducked into the hallway, disappeared down a stairwell, and was soon on the street, pushing it along behind him at a fast clip. His pace quickened as he approached a very familiar landmark in this strange city: the impressive brick edifice of the long-abandoned Boott Mills building. He passed by the half of the red brick building which had already been restored and converted to offices and apartments, and entered the other part, untouched for the better part of a century, inhabited only by shadows of its past. The man found his way through the dark with ease, because the building itself was quite familiar to him, even though its present surroundings were not. With light steps he slipped down the staircase to the lowest part of the building, near the conduits by which the water would in an earlier time have passed outside and back to the river, having delivered its share of power to the machinery above. Here it was wet and dark and cold, the foundation walls seeping with the silty sweat of the sluggish, dormant canals, the echo of the wild power of the river once harnessed to make mile after unending mile of cloth.

Here, in a location which he knew to be inconspicuous here and now, and also where he was going, he stopped and focused his thoughts, reaching out in that "other" direction as Wamesit had taught him. This was a spatial dimension unlike the familiar three, in that its entire extent was perhaps a quarter of an inch. But here, now, across that short span lay another world: in fact, the same world, but more than a century and a half in the past. That was actually his own time, and he had made this passage once already to get to this strange future, in which much of what was new and strange to him lay like a thin coat of paint over what had existed in 1842.

In the dark, he drew himself carefully across that narrow gap, keeping a hand over his knit cap to make sure it didn't blow off in the wind that might be blowing through on the other side. He knew that he had come safely across, though he was in the same dark damp sub-basement, because the building had suddenly become very much noisier, from the nonstop motion of the looms and the wheels and belts delivering power to them from the canal. The young man walked up stairs, now in a much newer-looking building, and emerged into the light of day. It hit him immediately, coming back to his familiar time, the Year of Our

Lord 1842: the Bells and the Smells. From a vantage point in front of the mill, he could survey both directions: eastward, toward the prim dormitories where the "mill girls" lived their chaperoned, protected lives when they were not at work, and the squalid slum to the west where the Irish laborers lived. The Irish had come into the area to build the system of canals for the mills of Lowell. The most backbreaking, dangerous, dirty and ill-paid of jobs were still theirs to do. As for the mills themselves, the gentlemen of the Boston Associates had made a conspicuous, and well-publicized, point of running their manufactures in a humane and Christian fashion, in contrast to the hellish exploitation for which the textile industry in Britain was widely criticized. To run the looms, they recruited young ladies from farm families in the local area. These "mill girls" would work for low wages, but their moral environment had to be assured in order to avoid meddling from the girls' families and, even worse, local ministers, who still wielded considerable political power. So every aspect of the girls' lives was protected, and regimented. Great bells atop the mills and the dormitories rang out to tell them when to arise, eat, go to work, take their breaks, pray, and so forth. Although they worked hard and had little freedom, for the most part the girls relished their independence and the unprecedented economic power their modest wages provided.

The Paddy Camps, as the two separate Irish slums along the Western Canal were commonly called, were a different story. They were a constant cause of concern among the high-minded Congregationalist farmers and merchants: a loud, stinking shambles of unruly and self-destructive behavior, as the steam constantly rising from the many homemade stills bore witness. To further justify the local farmers' dim view of the Irish, their ramshackle encampments had quickly sorted themselves into two hostile groups, those from Cork and those from Connaught. Random violence and pitched battles between the two factions were commonplace, and the establishment in 1831 of St. Patrick's Church, the first Catholic church in Massachusetts outside of Boston, did little to bring peace to the neighborhood, despite its deliberate location halfway between the two hostile camps. On the contrary, the church became the locus of power struggles, first between the two Irish camps, then between the laborers and the emerging Irish middle class which was establishing itself in a more respectable fashion on Chapel Hill.

Trudging through the nearer camp, the man heard familiar sounds: raucous laughter, screams and cries from a fistfight, the annoyed grunting of a sow being chased out of a bedroom. And, of course, the smell of open sewage was inescapable, mixing in with what would otherwise have been delightful aromas of stew and boiling cabbage. The young man especially noticed it after his brief visit to the other, future time. Not that their air was so good, but at least they were able to keep their shit out of the way, for the most part.

He sat for a moment on a stone bench by the Western Canal, not for rest (for his kind had little need of it) but to gather his thoughts. Wamesit had taken pains to make certain that he understood exactly how the portal worked, how such a thing was made possible, and why it was here in this place, connecting these particular times. Struggling to grasp concepts far beyond what any humans in the mid-19th century understood of the universe, Tin accepted that space and time might be oddly related aspects of the same flexible fabric upon which everything in the universe is printed, and that this fabric could be bent in such a way as to bring the same spatial locale (or, more accurately, a portion of the Earth's surface) into proximity with itself at a different time. But Tin marveled at the difficulty of keeping this connection stable, with the Earth spinning on its axis and careening at high speed in its orbit around the Sun, which in turn was dragging the Earth and the other planets in a long cyclical journey around the Galaxy. This "folding" must involve so much twisting and distortion, that surely there must be catastrophic side effects. Who could have done this? Surely not the Firsts: their substance, thoughts and powers were bound to the Earth. No, this pointed to other intelligences, abiding in the vast spaces between Earth and other worlds. Why? Why carry out this incredible manipulation of the Universe to tie together two specific years on the planet Earth? And how can Wamesit be so certain that this is a means of defeating the Demon?

Though he carried out his duty as he must, the thought of traveling between times disturbed Tin on a deep moral level. If it was possible for someone to travel backward in time and change everything that was ordained to occur from that earlier time forward, then Reality itself was a mockery, and there was no purpose or value in what anyone thought, did, or experienced.

And it also made possible the existence of things or events which occurred because in some way they had traveled backwards in time and caused themselves to occur (like becoming one's own grandfather, for example) . Such events would be "uncaused" or "uncreated", and the unfolding of the Universe would be equally consistent with or without them. Such things were not so threatening, but Tin viewed them as ugly pimples on the face of Reality: disgusting. He had to use this time passage to accomplish his mission, which was undeniably important, but he didn't have to like it.

Tin decided to set these questions aside for the moment, since he was unlikely to get answers, or need answers, soon. Like all Thirds, he was practical-minded, but also had a vital need to have his philosophy, values and view of the world clearly in order, so that he might use his formidable powers, swiftly and without restraint, in any situation that might arise. The time passage was a tool provided him in the furtherance of his mission, and he understood his mission reasonably well.

His musings having reached a dead end, Tin gathered himself up and walked the remaining few steps to the back of St. Patrick's church, and entered a modest office containing a small desk and a serious-looking middle-aged man with prematurely white hair.

"Mister Healey, I have returned from that time in the future, more than a century and a half hence", he said to the man, as he sat down in a small wooden chair. "The signs are unmistakable: in this time, the Demon is becoming more active. It appears to have plans in motion, and confederates who are not completely mad or imbecile."

Charles Healey spoke. "As I feared, your report has confirmed the predictions of the Bashaba. I was hoping for a different outcome, but now our task is here laid before us. Have you found our Talents there?"

The young man replied, "I met two who have the Light in abundance, and are clearly the ones we seek. One of them is a son of the Soil, Irish like yourself. Whether there is any Irish left in the soul in that time is not at all clear. The remarkable thing about him is that he has been single-mindedly pursuing the hidden truth about the world, and has come amazingly close to it, by a purely intellectual path. He does not bear the sign of having been 'touched' by any First or Second. The other, you may be surprised to hear, is from the land of Brazil. There are many such residing in the city in that future time, and they appear to occupy a place in society not unlike that which your countrymen do in this time. The young woman of whom I speak has such a power in her, it is amazing that those around her are not blinded by the light of it. Yet she seems unaware. I actually spoke with her at one point. I was being attacked by some young men who were unwittingly working on the Demon's behalf, and was trying to figure out how to escape without revealing myself, when this girl apparently frightened them all away by pointing some kind of communication device at them."

He continued, "I also felt the presence of another Talent in the city, a well-intentioned one who actually knows much of the truth and should be working with us. I believe that he knew of my presence and avoided me."

Charles Healey thought about this for a moment, and said with a sly look, "And what of yourself? Did you meet yourself in that time? What are you up to then?"

"Sir, you mock me. It is most unbecoming of a man of your position".

"What, an Irish elf who has lost his sense of humor? Did it go over the side along with your dinner on the voyage? What a dreadful calamity!"

Tin went red in the face, but controlled his anger, reminded yet again of Healey's general suspicion of Tin and his kind. The human was bound by duty and necessity to accept Tin's help, but too many stories from his homeland (unfortunately, many of them true) led him to believe the worst. Tin decided to address the issue forthrightly, once again, for all the good that it would do.

"Sir, you know, or think you know, what I am. But you also know my purpose full well, and that this purpose was provided by the same One who provided yours. And if you know anything at all about my kind, you may confidently assume that every part of my strength and acumen are devoted to that purpose, and that along the way I will not be stealing infants, or turning people into donkeys, or any of that other nonsense."

Healey replied, "As reasonable as that surely is, it means nothing, since surely your most fundamental talent would be that of making your intent seem reasonable and wholesome. What counts for more is that you have the confidence of all of those in whom I trust. Every day I pray that their confidence is well placed."

Tin sighed. "Each day we have that day's work before us, so as long as we understand what that work is, let us concentrate ourselves on it, and not be distracted by thoughts of things which by their very nature are unknowable. At the end of that road lies paralysis and feeblemindedness, as you know full well.

"Now, what shall I do about the two talents that I have located, while the other remains hidden?"

Healey replied, "We need a gathering of minds, and soon. Go fetch the two that you have located, even if you cannot find the other one. Then we must have a talk with the Bashaba. The other one will no doubt show himself upon your return, at which time our new friends may explain things to him. He will help, or he will not. We can wait no longer."

Tin was thrilled at the prospect. The Bashaba is a truly remarkable human, he thought. What effect will he have on these two, who are so close to realizing their powers? It will be a fascinating meeting indeed, for everyone involved.

Chapter 5

Flashback (1 year before the present) in which a Nasty Man meets the God of his Choice

The sky was grey with clouds, and it was quiet along the river except for the rustling of a light breeze through the bushes on either bank. From far upstream the idle chugging of a boat engine became audible. Around the riverbend the boat came into view: just a small craft with a couple of fishing poles along the side. It carried a couple of friends out for a pleasant weekend boat ride, perhaps catching a fish or two. It was late Sunday afternoon, and this was the only boat still out on this part of the river.

With shocking suddenness, the surface of the water became very turbulent immediately around the boat. It had the appearance of two perfectly synchronized whirlpools on either side of the small vessel. Before any of the passengers aboard even had time to become alarmed, the boat was yanked down under the surface as if it had been grasped by a giant hand. The water covered over the space where the boat had just been, perfectly smooth now, as if the boat had never been there at all. No wake, no waves, no sound.

All this was witnessed by only one person. Oswald Benson, a homeless drug addict, had spent most of the afternoon sitting in the weeds on the riverbank, aimlessly watching the river and riding out the high from the heroin he had shot around noon. He had ventured upriver a bit, all the way to the Middlesex Village neighborhood, where he would be less likely to be beaten up.

Of course, most people would be inclined to give him a wide berth if they spotted him there on the riverbank. He was of medium height, with his second-hand clothes hung loosely on his scrawny frame, and his greasy reddish-brown hair pulled back into a ragged ponytail. His thin mustache drooped down on either side of his mouth, Lemmy-style, a look that he considered kind of cool and menacing. The menacing effect, such as it was, was helped along a little by the fact that the heroin had already begun its long, slow work of causing his teeth to fall out. All of these various "fashion choices", and his vague but sneery expression, marked him clearly as Someone to be Avoided, as he seemed equally likely to pull a knife and rob you, or to suddenly die messily right in front of you, or perhaps one and then the other, just to maximize the general unpleasantness of the encounter.

Oswald had watched the boat drift downstream from Tyngsborough and stop to set some fishing lines, then get abruptly sucked underwater. He was just lucid enough to recognize that this was unusual, and found it quite interesting. He felt an instinctive empathy and admiration for whatever it was that had done this. He had no sympathy for the victims on the boat, or for people in general for that matter. Oswald had the unshakeable belief that he had made all the right choices in life, and his current troubles were the result of a persistent unfairness, a generalized injustice that must be set right by any means that came within his limited grasp. His daily experience suggested that the conspiracy was very widespread. The people he had to rob and burglarize just to get by were no end of trouble, to start with. Then, the dealers loved to jerk him around, always late when they knew he needed a fix the most. And getting from one to the other often involved passing a gauntlet of vicious young men with fast-moving fists and feet, who always seemed to know when he had money. At the free food kitchen there was another host of problems. Some of those guys really were bums (unlike Oswald), and would try and grab all the best food on purpose just before Oswald got to it. The fat stupid brain dead slobs. No matter. Oswald knew that he was destined for greatness, and one day would have a nice big car that he could use to run over all these people, and enjoy the sound of their bones snapping under his wheels. These were the dreams that helped get him through his ragged days.

Oswald continued to stare at the water where the boat had gone down, still thrilled at what he had just seen. A strange idea got into his head, an idea that was too powerful to resist. He stood up and walked straight down the bank and into the water, hardly noticing how cold it was. He continued wading into the river, straight toward the center, continuing even after he was entirely under water. Somehow this didn't seem to matter, and he felt as though he was breathing normally. Having gone a few hundred feet, he sensed that he was at the midline of the riverbed. And although the water was murky here at the bottom, and though the light of day was fading, he could see with unnatural clarity a great distance upriver and down. What he saw served to amplify the thrill he felt at watching the helpless boaters sink to their deaths. For, as far as he could see in either direction, along the center of the riverbed, there was a long line of boats of various types, all showing hull damage as though they had been squeezed by a giant hand. And on many of them he could see either the bare skeletons of their passengers, or their partially decomposed bodies. Oswald had formed the impression from movies and TV shows that drowned bodies always floated to the top eventually (unless they had cement overshoes, ha ha). But he was quite sure that none of these people would ever leave the river bottom.

He turned and walked back to the riverbank, as a whole universe of new thoughts filtered into his mind. He was becoming, not a new person, but a better, more effective version of the person he had been. There was a cost, and an obligation, but it hardly mattered since he would richly enjoy every one of the tasks that he would be required to carry out. He stepped out of the river and back onto the bank where he had been sitting, contemplating the new life that had been given him by the terrible, wonderful being in the river. In his distracted state he hardly noticed that his clothes were still completely dry. He had important things to do now. He needed to find a person named Moss, who would give him the detailed knowledge and instructions he needed. He had a vague idea of where he would find this person, and a confident belief that they would meet very soon.

As his sickly frame pulsed with the thrill of newfound strength and clarity, he realized still more things with an uncanny certainty. He knew that the food he scrounged from garbage cans and dumpsters would never make him sick again. Maybe soon he wouldn't even have to get food from those places anymore. A while later he would notice that his craving for heroin had vanished. Still filled with rapture as he pissed on a nearby culvert, he thought to himself, I need to have a name for you, O great one! What is your name? The answer, if you could call it that, was a feeling as though a large hammer had struck his skull from the inside. He staggered from the blow, and got some urine on his pants as a result. Oh well, not exactly the first time. Not even the first time today. And off he strode towards the downtown area. He had a picture in his mind of his destination: Lowell City Hall. Under any normal circumstances, this would be a place to avoid, situated next to police headquarters at JFK Plaza. But this was a new world, and everything would be different now.

In his filthy clothes, he drew a few stares as he entered City Hall, but made his way to the 4th floor without any opposition, and navigated the hallways to the office to which the image in his mind was leading him. The lettering on the door said "Wilkins – Planning Board". It did not occur to him that it was odd that City Hall should be open, and someone actually working in the offices, on a Sunday afternoon. Benson entered the office, which was jammed with file cabinets and very old-fashioned office furniture. Seated behind a massive mahogany desk was a small man with a wizened face and… pointed ears. This was strange, as was the fact that he was looking for a man named Moss in an office belonging to someone named "Wilkins". But he had to go through with this, whatever it was. "Umm, I am looking for… Moss?" he asked the odd creature behind the desk.

The small old man leaped up from his desk, rushed over and shut the office door. "Quiet, you idiot!" was the response. "Do not mention that name here, or anywhere! My name is Wilkins, and that is how you will address me. What took you so long? I was expecting you half an hour ago."

Benson's fear and bewilderment expressed itself as petulance. "Look, for one thing, I had to walk, and for another, the most direct route goes through some places that I really need to avoid. Anyway, who are you and how did you know I was coming? And what exactly is going on?"

The older man paced around his office as he spoke. "I know that you had an encounter with our big friend in the water. Your name is Oswald Benson, and until roughly an hour ago you were homeless, and a heroin addict. Now you are neither. What is more, you are about to become a rather important local religious figure.

"I can tell you that the thing in the water is a God, or as close to a God as you'll ever want. It is very powerful, and generally not in a good mood. You see what sort of things It does to people for no particular reason. Try to imagine what It does to people who hear Its call, and do not help It get what It wants.

"So, as I said, It is a God, and in fact It is the greatest of the Gods. All the other ones got jealous and ganged up on It, and trapped It in the place you just came from. What It wants is… escape. It is stuck in that part of the river, upstream of the falls, and must somehow reach the ocean in order to reclaim Its full power. What happens when It finally gets out is no concern of yours, or mine for that matter." There was a brief twitch in Wilkins' face, as though he had felt, or merely anticipated, a sudden pain, but this passed as he continued.

"I have been trying to work out a way to accomplish this for several centuries. We nearly made it in 1842, but the path was not sufficiently clear. I have been preparing since then for another attempt, which will not have the same difficulties. That is where you come in.

"We will be making this attempt in about a year. The physical preparations are nearly complete, but when the time comes we will need to have a number of things happen precisely on schedule in various parts of the city. This will require a lot of people doing things that are dangerous, illegal, and completely stupid, simply because we tell them to. Now what is the quickest and easiest way to arrange that, I ask you?"

It was all Benson could do to try and keep up with this torrent of new information, and all he could think of to say was, "Uhhh…..?"

Wilkins was clearly not in a patient frame of mind. "A cult, dumbass! We will start a cult here in Lowell, and you will be its Messiah, you moron! Don't worry, I will tell you what to say and do every step of the way. You just concentrate on delivering it all with conviction and showmanship. You were great in your high school musical, and you should have no trouble with this"

"You saw that? Eighteen years ago? Who the hell are you?" This was a little too weird. He could barely remember that far back himself. How much did this creature know about him? Everything, it would appear. Could he trust him? It seemed that he had no choice.

Benson managed to pull himself together enough for one seemingly relevant question. "And what's with the ears? Who goes around in public with fake pointy ears on?"

"Fake? Hardly. Take a good look at me. Go on, a really good look"

As Benson tried to focus and concentrate, all of a sudden the man's ears looked normal, and the man himself didn't look nearly as old. He said, "This is the way everyone else sees me. My work requires considerable day to day contact with humans, and my true appearance would cause obvious difficulties."

After saying this, he once again looked the way he had when Benson first came in the office: like a man who was 500 years old or more, in perfect health, with pointed ears. He continued, "You have been given the ability to see people like me in their true form. This is very important for the work that you will be doing. If you see any others like me, you must assume that they are working against us, and you and your followers must kill them. They are not easy to kill, but you must do your best.

"As you gather your followers, some of them will form your core group, the most easily manipulated of the bunch. We will grant them the gift of true sight as well, and they too will be commanded to kill any others of my sort that they see. We'll make up a reason that they'll accept. Needless to say, none of these people will be allowed to see me. It won't be a problem, since I rarely leave this building."

Benson was starting to like the sound of this. Maybe I'll like doing what this guy says, he thought. With a feeling of eager anticipation, he asked "So how do I start?"

He had correctly guessed that this "interview" was at its end. Wilkins produced a hotel card key, handed it to Benson, and replied, "You start by taking this over to the Doubletree Hotel. This is the key to your luxury suite, which is where you will live until your Belvidere mansion is ready. Try not to be seen by too many people when you go there the first time: you look like hell, and you smell even worse than you look. The first thing you will do there is clean yourself up. Six or seven long hot showers ought to do the trick. Throw out the clothes you are wearing: you will find plenty of clothes already in the room, in your size. We will arrange for a dentist, hair stylist, manicure and pedicure over the next couple of days. In your suite you will find a binder with your name on it. It contains the details of the religious philosophy which you will preach as the basis of your cult, and has dates, places and times for you to get this under way. This is your "revelation". Study it, learn it, absorb it, and study it some more. You need to understand this as thoroughly as if it was your idea in the first place, and as if you actually believed it. It's actually quite novel and interesting, and is just the thing to get the attention of plenty of impressionable humans.

"And just keep one thing firmly in mind. Disobey me in even the smallest detail, and I can promise you a long life of such misery that you will look back on your days as an addict as a happy memory. Now go."

As Benson turned to leave, he had an amazing insight. The old creep doesn't know, he thought to himself. Apparently Moss/Wilkins did not know something that Benson did: that the release of the Being into the ocean would bring about the end of the world. To Oswald Benson, that prospect was thrilling. His feeling was, he cared for the world about as much as the world cared for him, which was not at all. And this would show them all, it really would. He hoped that somehow, when it happened, everyone in the world would know that he, Oswald Benson, had been on the winning team, that he had been an important part of making it happen.

In the meantime, he had a lot to look forward to. Cult leader? Those dudes have it made. Their followers will do anything for them. Maybe one of them will throw himself in front of a bus, just because I told him to. That would be so cool. Can't do it too often, it would probably attract attention, and the old shriveled guy would get mad. But maybe just once or twice. And then there were the women to consider. Bring in a few good looking ones who would do anything he said, and maybe Oswald wouldn't want the world to end quite so soon…

Anyway you sliced it, this was definitely going to be the best job he had ever had (although, admittedly, there hadn't been many to form the basis for comparison). Oswald was quite energized as he maneuvered his filthy self out of City Hall and headed over to the hotel to get started on this fine, though short, new life.

Chapter 6

In which the same Nasty Man does Something Amazing

Bea was riding the bus from the PC shop in the Highlands to her home in the Chapel Hill neighborhood, holding on to the rail as the bus lurched over the broken pavement. After the strange events of the early morning, and her unnerving attack of melancholy, the rest of the day had gone smoothly. She always had an easy time working with computers: they always seemed to cooperate with whatever she needed to do. Even when a customer had done something stupendously dumb to mess their system up, Bea could always get to the bottom of the problem and restore it to working order, usually better than it was before. After all, it was just code. Very often she would simply ask the computer to retrace its steps, which was usually sufficient to recover supposedly unrecoverable files and registry settings. She found that computers could be shown how to do this themselves, and once she had loaded one of her special programs, they would happily do as she asked. Computers were so much easier to deal with than people most of the time.

She was looking forward to dinner, although she knew that her mother wouldn't be home. Mãe would have stopped at home, between her daytime housecleaning job and her night shift at the donut place, to cook some feijoada, which she would leave for Bea and Carolina. Brazilians liked to joke about feijoada, but as far as Bea was concerned, if you had to eat the same thing every day there could be no better choice. It was cheap, nutritious and relatively easy to prepare, and her mother's was much better than what they made at the local restaurants.

She got off the bus at the end of her block, walked up the sidewalk and up the short walkway to the front entrance of her apartment building, to the first floor apartment she shared with her mother and sister. She could smell the feijoada as she went inside, but surprisingly, her mother was at home, sitting at the kitchen table, looking very tense.

"What's up, Mãe? Why aren't you at work?"

"Thank God you're here, Beazinha! You have to talk to your sister! It's terrible!" Bea now saw that her mother's eyes were red from crying.

"What did Carolina do?" This sounded distressing. Mãe was normally so complacent about anything that happened in this country. Consequently, Carolina had gotten away with a lot of things that she shouldn't have in the last few years. Any time her mother would question something Carolina wanted to do, she would claim that "that's the way things are done here", and her mother would have no answer to that.

"It's terrible! She's dropped out of school, and she's joined that awful cult! The way she spoke to me, I don't even know her anymore! Beazinha, you are so smart, please talk some sense into her! Please, I don't know what to do…".

Carolina had done some upsetting things in recent years, but this really sounded serious. "Don't worry, Mãe, I will do everything I can. You should get to work now, don't risk getting into trouble. I am sure it must be some silly idea Lina has gotten into her head, and it should be easy enough to get it back out again."

Reluctantly, her mother gathered her things and left for her second job. Bea, with dinner forgotten, headed into the bedroom she shared with her sister. Carolina was lounging on her bed, with an air of nonchalance that Bea could see was faked.

"So, Lina, what's it this time? And when should we expect the police at our door?"

"Bea, it's not like that at all! It's wonderful! You should be a part of it too!"

"Well, Lina, it's a bit too late for me to drop out of high school and ruin my life, and I don't enjoy upsetting Mãe the way you do."

"No, no, no, you don't understand, Bea. Father Oswald has an amazing message, he reveals the way things really are, and it's totally liberating! None of that other bullshit matters, I need to follow him and get closer to God."

Carolina sounded very serious. In fact, she sounded more mature than she usually did. Bea decided to try the Socratic approach, if only because she really needed more information. If she was supposed to avoid this Oswald character, as the little elf-guy had insisted, it would certainly help to learn more about him.

"All right, Lina, I'll bite. What's this Oswald and his 'message' all about?"

"Okay, Bea, I'll try to explain it all. But please be patient, I want to make sure I get it all right.

"You know how the Hindus have this idea of reincarnation? That souls move from one life to another, and go to a better or worse life depending on how well they behaved in the previous one? Well, Father Oswald has discovered that the Hindus have this only partly right. Souls move from life to life all right, but there is really only one soul. You see, God created the universe in order to experience it fully. So God actually does live every life in Creation, because God is the mind and soul of every being that has ever lived or ever will live. God has to go back and forth in time in order to do this, but hey, why not?

"So, why would God need to be rewarded or punished for living one of God's lives? Who is supposed to do the rewarding or punishing? That's not the way it works. Instead, after every life the soul gets better and smarter, and its next existence is automatically better, no matter what. We're all the same soul, you see? And every one you meet is actually you, either before or after your life, and we are all God.

"Father Oswald has figured this out because he is the Last. His is the last life that God has to live. That means Oswald's soul has the benefit of every living thing's life experiences, including yours and mine, including things that haven't even happened yet! Isn't that incredible?

"And it's important to know where you are in the sequence. Father Oswald says that there are those who will hear his message and ignore it. That's OK, they are farther back and not ready to understand. There are also those who hear his message and accept it, and those are the ones that are farther ahead. The farthest ahead of all are the ones who pretty much understand his message without him even having to explain it. Those people are really amazing."

Bea was hardly in any mood for any more mind-blowing events, but this sounded like a very nasty scam, and Carolina needed to see that. "Lina, just because some guy says that he's the next best thing to God, that doesn't mean you automatically believe it. People say all sorts of crazy things all the time, and usually they're just after your money."

"Bea, you have always thought I was stupid, but I'm not! I wouldn't believe what Father Oswald says just because he says it. He can do… amazing things. Things that only someone who was close to completing God's experience of Creation could do."

"Like what?"

"Come with me tonight and you'll see. There is a service by the river at 9:00. Come with me. It will open your eyes. I want you to see the truth, Bea, it's important!"

"Lina, if you think that this nonsense is more important than school, I can't stop you, but when you find yourself at the police station, don't expect any help from me. I'll tell them I don't even know who you are. And I have often thought you were a pain in the ass, but I never thought you were stupid. Until tonight."

Carolina looked sincerely shocked, as though she had actually expected Bea to go along with all of this. To be honest, Bea was mostly scornful of this metaphysical babble, but was at least a little bit spooked. That little man this morning had specifically warned her that this 'Father Oswald' was dangerous, and the boys that were trying to kill him were apparently doing this on Oswald's instructions. Bea was troubled and confused, but had made up her mind what to do before Carolina angrily left the apartment.

Beatrisa waited a few minutes before following, intending to do so without Carolina seeing her. Tapping her foot, she glanced over at the framed picture on the dresser, of herself and Carolina at the Folk Festival last year. Sometimes, when she was feeling particularly down on herself, Bea would catch herself thinking that, as far as appearance went, she was the practice run, and Carolina was the finished product. There was no doubt that Carolina was attractive, with a slim figure, almond-shaped face, perky nose, big bright eyes and shiny hair, but even in her worst moments, Beatrisa could not envy her little sister. Especially since Carolina was so messed up, so much of the time. It couldn't be easy, being her.

After a sufficient time had passed, Beatrisa left the apartment herself and followed her sister, hoping not to be discovered. Fortunately, it wasn't that difficult. Carolina strode purposefully through the downtown streets, oblivious to the dangerous areas, and was apparently too focused to notice anything, her older sister included. As for Bea, although she was quite focused on not losing track of Carolina, she was too alert to be surprised by the sort of trouble that awaited in any of the shadows adjoining the downtown neighborhoods.

Soon enough, she saw Carolina heading towards a crowd of people at the riverside park, just at the foot of the hill below UMass Lowell's south campus. Bea slowed down and found a spot in which she could observe without being seen. She saw a middle-aged guy in white robes, and although she couldn't make out what he was saying, his audience certainly was enthralled. He was speaking to them from a short pier on the river, where you would expect a couple of boats to be tied up. There were no boats there now, just (she assumed) "Father Oswald". As he spoke, she saw Carolina near the front of the audience, and also Roberto and the thugs that were with him this morning.

This was strange. Bea recognized this 'Father Oswald'. Not as a hokey preacher, but as a dirty bum. One time, a couple of years ago, she had chased this guy off as he was urinating in the alley behind Rudy's shop. Of course, he looked different now in some ways: cleaner, in white robes that must have come from some Halloween shop, and with some missing teeth replaced. But those same eyes were there, with their dead fire. She found those eyes creepy when he was a bum. She found the sight of all these people paying worshipful attention to him thoroughly depressing. Carolina should not be listening to this person: she should not be within a mile of him! She recognized some other people in the crowd besides her sister and Roberto. These are not stupid people, she thought. What does he have that could interest them?

After a short sermon, Oswald and the crowd went silent. Everyone was still watching him intently, as he strode to the end of the pier, and……… walked out across the surface of the water. He went out about a hundred feet, turned around, and lifted his arms like he was Charlton Heston in "The Ten Commandments". There was apparently no formal ceremony to this, but his audience all reacted, either applauding, raising their hands to the sky, or moaning in what they must have imagined was some kind of spiritual rapture.

Bea had already experienced some uncanny things today, and was ready to believe in a few unbelievable things, but this just looked like a cheesy trick. How could even Carolina (who, although Bea loved her dearly, might not be the sharpest knife in the drawer) be taken in by this?

The answer came moments later, as Oswald returned to the pier, and motioned for some of his followers, Carolina included, to join him. Each one in turn went for the same walk out across the surface of the water, holding Oswald's hand as if that was what was keeping them from sinking. That must be a whole lot harder to fake, Bea thought. And the sight of it disturbed her more than she wanted to admit to herself. It must be a trick, but she couldn't see how it could possibly work. And she was accustomed to seeing how things worked, always. What if it was real? What if it was real? Strange things are going on. If a little man who knows my name can get beaten to death and jump right back up again without a scratch, then what's real and what isn't? One thing hadn't changed from this morning, at least: if she was scared at the idea of "Father Oswald" based on this morning's events, she was very much more scared at the reality. It wasn't even so much the trick of walking on the water. From a distance, and without the distraction of hearing whatever it was that he was saying, she had formed an impression of the man himself. He was utterly, transparently, insincere, and yet had a self-confidence that seemed unearthly, as if he was absolutely certain that his message would be convincing, even though he himself knew it was complete rubbish. And the look he had as he took Carolina out across the water, Bea did not like that look at all. The old lech was leering at her in greedy anticipation, and didn't seem to care who saw it.

The "ceremony" ended and the crowd walked off in all directions. Beatrisa emerged from her hiding place and tried to blend in with the people heading away towards School Street. She overheard a couple of young men talking. One said "Hey, nobody died this time. What gives?" The other replied, "You know Father Oswald is smart. He's the Last One, he has to be smart, right? Well, there are a bunch of new people in the congregation, and Oswald probably doesn't want to scare them off before they get to understand What's What."

"Still, it was cool to wonder who was going to get pulled under in that walk across the river. I mean, it's not as though getting killed is such a bad thing, right? Not when you know you're coming back as something better? It just means that they're going to get along to the next step a bit sooner, that's all."

"I don't suppose you're in a big hurry to 'move on'?" Teased the second one.

"No, I have to admit, I must not be that evolved. Still, it's wicked cool to watch."

Bea had heard and seen enough, more than enough. That strange little guy this morning had said that this Oswald was dangerous, and Bea could see all too clearly that this was true. She circled back towards the riverfront, to intercept Carolina on her way back. But she did not see her among the people walking east along Pawtucket. Moving closer to the park itself, she saw that the group had already dispersed completely, no sign of Oswald or his admirers. Breaking into a run, she checked what remained of the crowd going west and south into the UMass Lowell campus, and north across the bridge. There was no way that Carolina, on foot, could have gotten away from there without Bea seeing. There had been a few cars parked in the little dirt parking lot, and along the street. Carolina must have left in one of those.

Bea realized that she had made a big mistake in leaving Carolina out of her sight for those few minutes. She told herself that this was just one of Carolina's annoying stunts, that she had gone off with some other kids to some wild party, and would stumble back home at some late hour, feeling sick and ashamed. There was no way that she would have gone away with that terrible man. It just didn't make sense. Carolina simply could not be involved in something like this. Bea would explain it to her tonight. Carolina would see. Bea could always get Carolina to see what was right. It was going to be OK.

Carolina did not come home that night.

****

Back at City Hall, Wilkins appeared to be working late as usual. No one else who worked at City Hall had ever seen him leave the building (at least not in the last hundred years), but people tended to get confused on the rare occasions when they thought about him, and usually ended up assuming that they had seen him arriving at work and leaving work like anyone else, just putting in longer hours.

He didn't actually have any City business on his desk at the moment, he was just enjoying the thought of Benson's "miracle", which he knew was taking place at that moment. That guy has done well for such an unimaginative, brain-damaged sociopath, he thought. Well, obviously he was the right man for the job. With my script, his delivery, and a little assistance from You Know Who, he's well on his way to gathering a nice little obedient army of losers. It was so easy to fill their little minds with that self-flattering mumbo jumbo. Actually, that "one recycling soul" business was quite clever. You would think that a belief like that would induce humans to be exceptionally kind to one another, and exceptionally tolerant and understanding of the behavior of others. And, if it had been presented in a different way, it might have had that effect. But with the spin that he and Oswald put on it, it was calculated to make people amoral, self-absorbed, insufferably conceited, reckless, and abjectly dependent on Oswald for their self-esteem. So far it seemed to be working extremely well. These people would have no qualms about stealing explosives, setting them off in residential areas, or blocking police and fire department vehicles with their bodies. Very good! They will undoubtedly be a little let down when they find out that all this metaphysical business was just to get them to do this one thing, this one time. But if it all goes as planned, they won't have much time to feel let down, because very soon after, they will all be.....

!!!!!!!!!!!!!!!! Another terrible headache, so painful that Wilkins lost his train of thought and momentarily forgot who he was and where he was. There were some things he must never think about, or even think about thinking about. Wilkins slumped in his chair from the pain, and was sliding to the floor as he heard a knock on the door, which had been open. A black man carrying a computer CPU. A short man, with a genial expression and a head as round as a bowling ball. He was dressed in a cheap suit with a bright floral tie: obviously a man who did not take formal attire very seriously. It was that genial expression that bothered Wilkins: it made the man difficult to read. But he was still in pain, and didn't need to waste his mental energy on every trivial human who crossed his path, so he decided to let this go.

"Excuse me sir, do you need any help?" The man was Jamaican, judging by the accent. "I'm sorry about the late hour, but I was told that you needed your system upgrade as soon as possible, even if it required a night delivery".

Oh, it was the PC repair guy. OK, no problem. Don't show weakness in front of humans.

"No thanks, I was reaching for a pencil that I dropped. Sorry if it looked like I was in trouble. I would like that new system hooked up now, if you don't mind. Please take care of it while I take a break".

Rudy Foster watched the old man walk down the hall. He had tried to be careful not to let on that he could see the man's pointed ears, and hoped that he had been careful enough. This one appeared to be paranoid and on edge. Anyway, that was a strange tableau that he saw as he came in. The old creature was clearly in pain. It must require something extraordinary to cause that. Anyway, this confirmed his suspicion that there was a supernatural being of some kind in City Hall. That was why he had gone to great lengths to get the upgrade contract, bidding so low that his shop would be losing quite a bit of money. It appeared that Wilkins didn't want to be seen right now. Very good, time to take advantage. The man had left his old PC on, and obviously Rudy was expected to transfer all its programs and files to the new one. This was straightforward, and Rudy started an automated process (devised by Bea, actually) to accomplish the transfer through a USB cable. This would be an excellent opportunity to do some snooping, except that the old man didn't appear to be keeping any sensitive files, or anything of any substance, on his computer. It still made sense to load a "snitch" routine, that would send an encoded record of everything done on this computer to an anonymous folder on a web server, which only Rudy could access. This would be completely inconspicuous, riding on antivirus updates, clock corrections, email, or anything else that would normally occur as "overhead" over a network connection. This was actually not one of Bea's creations: he would not have wanted to explain to her why he wanted it. He had paid good money to a hacker for this particular bit of software.

While the PC transfer was happening, Rudy found the papers on Wilkins' desk a little more interesting. There were some very old, faded folders whose labels suggested that they dealt with the maintenance of the canal system in the city. That was odd: canal maintenance was the responsibility of that Italian energy firm which had acquired the Proprietors of Locks and Canals company. What interest did the Planning Board have in that? Also, and more ominous, he saw copies of requisitions for dynamite and other excavation supplies. Again, same question: what did the Planning Board need with explosives? Rudy was careful not to touch any of these papers or files.

Just as he was completing the setup of the new PC, Wilkins came back down the hall and into his office. Rudy thought he saw Wilkins make a very quick scan of the room to see what had been disturbed. Rudy was seized with a sudden panic: an innocent, disinterested person probably would have touched or shifted something at random. Would it look suspicious that he hadn't? Too late to do anything about it.

"The upgrade is all finished, Sir. Would you like me to dispose of the old CPU?"

The old man looked annoyed, and said "No I would not like for you to go through all my files at your leisure, thank you very much! I will either wipe the hard drive with a large electromagnet or find a very deep well to toss it into. Either way, it's none of your business. If you're done, then leave."

"Very well, sorry if I offended. Have a good evening!" Rudy left without the old CPU, but with a great deal to think about.

Chapter 7

A Short Journey to a Distant Place

The blues were in the air that morning, and Ronald O'Malley had his share and more besides. He had gotten up early, feeling oddly uncomfortable in his apartment, and made the short walk over to the college. He was now in his office, way too early, since his first lecture of the day was not until midafternoon. That gave him plenty of time for brooding. A gloom gathered around him as he reflected on his career to date. It was either a stupendous success or a miserable failure, nothing in between. And the way he felt this morning, failure seemed a little closer to the truth. He had received many honors as a brilliant scholar, and had had promising positions at Harvard, MIT and Princeton. But that had little to do with his present situation.

The problem was, O'Malley was a collector of doctorates. He had successfully pursued postgraduate studies in each of a wide range of subjects, concentrating on each to the point of receiving a Ph.D. This would typically be followed by postdoctoral work, and sometimes an associate professorship. Then abruptly, he would abandon that field altogether, and start the very same process in a different field. In this manner, he had become a world-class expert in physics, paleobiology, archaeology, geology, the history of the New England region before and after the arrival of the European settlers, meteorology, and music. This had taken less time than one might expect, because when he was pursuing a subject, his focus was formidable, and he had been able to research and complete a solid thesis in each of these subjects in a remarkably short time.

Needless to say, he was driven by something other than a desire for a successful career. No wonder his wife had left him early on: he could imagine her frustration and disappointment. She thought he was mentally ill, and it was hard to argue with this. It was certainly an odd sort of attention deficit disorder that allowed a person the discipline and focus to complete a doctoral program. But the urge to move on once he had mastered the essentials of a field was overwhelming, and he kept on doing it , fully aware of how it damaged his career prospects. In a defensive mood, he could blame the way the academic system was structured, as if raw reality could be studied by limiting one's scope to narrow boxes, with no knowledge of or interest in other approaches. Well, people had been specializing that way for several hundred years now, with obvious success, so O'Malley couldn't even persuade himself that this attitude made sense.

There was perhaps another mental problem at work: maybe an obscure form of paranoia. O'Malley was convinced that randomness did not exist. The musical analogy he had presented to his lecture audience yesterday was in fact the central obsession of his life, and the driving force behind his zigzag scholarly career. Everywhere he went, he saw randomness that mocked him, in his conviction that the position of every pebble on the ground, every blade of grass, the shapes and motions of every leaf on every tree, the shapes of clouds, constituted a stream of information that, if he could only find a way to perceive it properly, would reveal meaning much more profound, and more significant, than the Ninth Symphony.

This was his belief and conviction, and though he had devoted enormous energies in its pursuit, at this moment he felt as far from the answers as he was on the day he was born. It was as though he had come to rest in this spot to fade away slowly. The community college administration liked the fact that he was able to teach so many subjects, even at the highest levels, and because of this were willing to indulge him in his strange cross-disciplinary seminars and research.

Fully occupied with feeling sorry for himself, he did not hear the young man enter his office, and was startled when the man spoke. “I know where you can find the music you are looking for, Professor”.

“Excuse me? Are you a student in one of my classes?” O’Malley had not actually absorbed the man’s statement. He looked up at the fellow. Was he actually young, or just small? It was hard to tell. He thought that he had seen him somewhere before, however.

“I am not an enrolled student, but I did attend your lecture yesterday afternoon. I found it a bit sad.”

“Sad? What do you mean?”

“I know what you are seeking, and it is as though you are scaling a mountain by the steepest and most difficult route possible. It might take several lifetimes to complete this quest. But there are shortcuts, and I think you are aware of some of the individuals in the past who have discovered these shortcuts.”

“I am also quite familiar with the B.S. of spiritualist con artists, so please don’t try to impress me that way.”

“Fair enough”, replied the small man. “By the way, I should introduce myself. My name is Tin. Of course, I already know who you are.”

“Well, that’s fine then, ‘Mr. Tin’. And just what can I do for you this morning?” O’Malley was getting a bit tired of this conversation.

It's time to wake this one up and get his attention, Tin thought. He waved in the direction of the wall, and said "Look upon the trivial for a moment…"

This did catch O'Malley's attention. He looked up and was transfixed. Gazing at his nondescript office wall, in an instant, based on its details, he had a vision of the construction of the building, the entire life experiences of all the carpenters, bricklayers and electricians, the sawmill and farm that occupied the site before the college was built, and further back, to the receding of the ice sheet thousands of years ago. All was implicit in the details right before him: anyone looking at this wall should be able to see it, and he could not understand why he never saw it before. Glancing down at his desk, he saw the rain forest where the mahogany came from, the factory where the saw was made that was used to cut down the tree, the workshop where the tools were made that were used to shape and assemble the desk, and further visions illuminating everything that had to do with the design, materials, construction, and even the delivery of the desk to this place.

O'Malley, overwhelmed, closed his eyes and shook his head. When he opened his eyes, the vision was gone. He was drenched in sweat, and panting as though he had just run a marathon. Amazed and confused, he looked questioningly at Tin. Tin answered the unspoken question, "It takes a lot out of you, doesn't it? You should be careful: a man your age could drop dead. But I need you to see something else. Look out your window. Do you see yonder cloud, the shape of its leading edge, the way it is moving against the other clouds?"

The Professor looked out his window. As before, what he was looking at was nothing out of the ordinary, just a few clouds moving lazily across the sky. But what he perceived in this sight struck him like a bolt of lightning. It was a few minutes before he could gather his wits enough to speak.

"I suspected something along these lines, but I had no idea they were so *old*!" he said.

Tin nodded. "Yes, they were alive and conscious on this world long before the first single-celled organisms swam in the oceans. And as you no doubt have also guessed, their thought processes, from the viewpoint of such creatures as you and I, are exceedingly slow. But they are also exceedingly subtle. This world of ours, this garden of life as we understand it, was created by them and in large part comprises their very substance. This world of ours is a garden, yes, but you may also look upon it as a message for those who might read it. As you have been trying to do with no assistance for all these difficult years. I am in awe of your courage, Sir, and I am more than delighted to be able to provide you with the reward you so deserve. And now that the door has been opened in your mind, you will be able to use this perception whenever you desire, subject to the limitations of your body. But I regret that I am also here seeking your help. There is a crisis brewing, with implications that will take some time to explain, and your insights may be crucial in determining a course of action. But to make things clear, I need you to take a short walk with me. We are just waiting for another vital member of the crew to arrive."

Bea was entering the building as he spoke. She had had a difficult night, a sleepless night, with worry increasing with every hour that Carolina did not appear. As the sunrise approached, Bea knew that Carolina was in trouble, and she was unsure what she could do about it. Go to the police? And tell them what exactly? That she knows that the leader of this strange religious group is actually a crazy bum, that he pulled some kind of unsavory black magic at the river, and that he is now likely to be doing some unspecified bad thing to her sister? And Bea had no evidence to convince the police that Carolina is even with those people: for all she knew Lina might have just stayed out drinking somewhere.

But Bea knew in her heart that this was not what Carolina had done at all, and that her sister was in real trouble. The only person she had met who seemed to see this Oswald character the same way she did was that strange elf-guy. His advice to her was to go see this Professor O'Malley at the community college. Well, at the very least she might be able to persuade him to get the police involved: the police tended to pay more attention to people like that.

Bea stepped tentatively down the hallway. She had audited a course in this building last year, so it was not completely unfamiliar. Even so, this early in the morning, with no one around, she felt very much out of place. What made it much worse was that O'Malley's office was on the third floor. It had taken all of her courage to get on the elevator and step out onto this floor, wondering how she could possibly explain herself if someone questioned her presence there. Ahead of her, at the end of the corridor, she saw light from an open office. She continued slowly toward it, and saw O'Malley's name on the door. Feeling suddenly ridiculous, but desperate for help at the same time, she peered shyly around the doorway. There was a man in his late forties sitting behind a desk, and the young man whom she had saved from a deadly beating just the previous morning. That was a relief, actually, since he seemed to know something about "Father Oswald".

The small man was the one who spoke. "Bem vindo, Beatrisa! Come in, please!" As she found a chair and sat down, he continued, "Since I know both of you, I will make the introductions. Professor O'Malley, this is Beatrisa DeSouza, an illegal alien from Brazil…" Bea felt a momentary pang of shock and fear at hearing this stated so crudely. "… and also a genius concerning your computing machines. And, Beatrisa, this is Ronald O'Malley, a brilliant scholar in many fields who has rejected success in order to pursue a truth that very few know, and none speak of openly." O'Malley, still in a daze from his expanded vision of a few moments ago, could not summon up any anger or resentment at this description, or any reaction whatever.

Beatrisa and O'Malley took a few awkward seconds to check each other out. Beatrisa saw a slightly overweight man with bushy, sandy hair that seemed ready to launch out in a variety of directions without any coordinated plan. His clothes were consistent with what she would expect from a college professor: a light blue cable turtleneck, no doubt expensive but a bit worn, with khaki pants and a very scuffed pair of loafers. He was also wearing a slightly dazed expression. Bea wondered whether something had just happened to prompt that look, or whether life in general kept him dazed on an ongoing basis.

For his part, O'Malley saw a short young woman, with a figure that might have been considered 'perfect' on someone about a foot taller. Her dark skin and black hair suggested that she might be Hispanic, but there was something about her that made him certain that she was Brazilian. He had seen young men and women from that country, at various shops and restaurants in the city, young adults whose deep reservoir of infectious cheer belied the fact that they had almost certainly seen more than their share of fear, loss and misery in their young lives. But, although he was certain that this girl was Brazilian, she did not quite fit the mold in some ways. For one thing, she was dressed for comfort rather than for looks, in an enormous baggy sweatshirt bearing the faded logo of an amusement park that had closed down years ago. And with her puffy cheeks and deep-set eyes, she could almost be described as "goggle-eyed", but that was not it exactly. With the lingering vestiges of the Sight, he recognized that she was someone who looked far more deeply into things than other people did, but that this seldom if ever brought her any joy.

They both turned their attention to the small man who had suddenly intruded into both of their lives, and, as if their vision was only now coming into focus, they suddenly noticed that the man had pointed ears, and clothes that seemed more in place in the 19th century than in the present.

Bea spoke up. "And what about you? Will you introduce yourself? Who, and what, are you?"

"My name is Tin. That's it, no last name. And as for what I am, I am sure that both of you can find a name for it in the folklore of your ancestors. A caution, Professor, you will not get a pot of gold for catching hold of me! I realize that I am not being totally forthcoming, but I will soon explain myself, and other things, more fully. Now to business!"

They both looked puzzled. What business?

"I would like both of you to come on a short walk with me, and talk with some friends of mine. Beatrisa, I promise that this will enable you to rescue your sister from the clutches of that awful charlatan this very day, and Professor O'Malley, this will reveal much more of the truth that you are seeking. These things I offer you, and rest assured that you will be able to help me with a very important matter as well."

As nonsensical as this might have sounded, Tin's sincerity and intensity were most convincing. In fact, Tin could make this promise to Beatrisa with complete assurance: he knew that he would be returning to his own time, and fully expected to live long enough to see this year again, in the proper fashion. In the unlikely event that the Bashaba found this young woman wanting for the task, Tin would take it upon himself, when he arrived at this year once again, to personally remove Beatrisa's sister from danger, and woe, dire woe be unto anyone who tried to prevent him from doing this.

Bea and O'Malley followed Tin out of the office, out of the building, around the corner and a few blocks down a side street to an old abandoned mill building. As he spoke, in tour-guide fashion, about the building itself, how it was built to make cloth on an unprecedented scale using the power of the river, they took the same path that Tin had taken the previous day, down the stairs to the spot near the great turbine itself, the dark sub-basement. He told them "Now this is where it gets tricky. We will pass through here. But you will need these when we come out again". From a bundle on the stone floor he handed each of them a thick, old-fashioned cloak, of a length that would cover them down to the ankles. He also handed each of them a pair of leather boots, saying "You will definitely need these, as those sneakers will not do at all." The boots appeared to be brand new, but intentionally scuffed to make them appear used, and were exactly the right size in both cases.

As before, Tin focused his mind and reached across that narrow gap separating the worlds. He instructed his guests to link hands, so that they would be able to move across as he did. They noticed the sudden change in temperature, and the sounds of the machinery, but did not think anything was terribly unusual in this, until they went back up the stairs, and outside into… a different world.

Chapter 8
In which Beatrisa is served Tea, and the Professor is Bonked on the Head

Beatrisa and Professor O'Malley stood amazed, viewing a street scene both familiar and unfamiliar. They were on the same street from which they had entered the abandoned mill, and all the buildings looked familiar, but the street was not paved and there were no cars on it. Come to think of it, some other things were missing, such as telephone lines and traffic lights.

Tin broke the momentary silence. "Please! Put your cloaks on, both of you!" It was at that point that they noticed that all of the people who were out on the street were dressed in a very old-fashioned way, as if this were a fantastically detailed movie set, or a vast historical re-enactment of some kind.

Tin continued, "Don't be afraid to accept the obvious. You are in Lowell but the year is 1842. Take a look: the mills are in full operation, powered by the water brought in by the canals. If you look around you will see some of the mill girls on their way from the boarding houses to the mills, and the Irish laborers working on the canals. You need the cloaks in order not to look outlandish in your clothes."

O'Malley said, "I can't believe that this is real, but it is fantastic! I am familiar with this time in Lowell's history, and everything looks the way I imagined it would. But, something must be wrong here. What is that smell?"

"Professor, that is the smell of a city without sewers. Yonder you can see the Paddy Camps, to whose residents your modern notions of sanitation and public health would be quite foreign. You will get used to the smell quickly. And yonder," he said, pointing to the southeast, "is Chapel Hill, where the more prosperous Irish folk live. And, of course, it is also where you live, Beatrisa, in your time."

Bea was not terribly disoriented by this change of scene. She had studied local history in school, so for the most part she understood what she was seeing. The city actually did not look that different. But her attention was being pulled in many directions: the interesting scene before her eyes, how they had been brought to this time, what sort of creature was Tin and what did he actually want from them, and foremost, how this was going to help Carolina.

As if reading her mind, Tin said, "Of course you want to know why I have brought you back to this time. I will explain everything shortly. In about two hours we will be joining an esteemed colleague of mine, and taking a carriage ride to speak with a person who is revered by all of us for his wisdom. This is vital because… the end of the world is close at hand, and the two of you may be the only ones capable of preventing it. I say that the end of the world is nigh, and it appears to be so in this time. The fact that the world is still intact in your time is irrelevant: the calamity I speak of will affect both times together. It is difficult to explain, but ponder the simple fact that we just made this passage from your time to this, and it may become clearer.

"Now, I have preparations to make. I encourage both of you to explore the city of this time, become familiar with it, and try to come to grips with what you have experienced. Meet me back at this location in two hours. They ring the bells atop the mills every half hour, so you should have no trouble keeping track. And please be careful!"

With that, Tin was off at a run, heading towards St. Patrick's Church. Bea and O'Malley stood awkwardly for a moment. The two of them were strangers suddenly thrown into a totally implausible situation. Whatever they had in common, though it might be obvious to Tin, was not at all obvious to them. Bea said, "Professor, I definitely want to check out the downtown area and Chapel Hill in the time we have available. I would expect that you have some places you are interested in looking at more closely. Don't worry about me: I will not get into any trouble. Let's just both learn all we can before we get dragged into something even stranger."

O'Malley agreed to this, and headed west, toward the Paddy Camps, while Bea strolled, slowly at first, past the boarding house. In the courtyard beside the boarding house, in front of the mill, she saw a young girl, perhaps twelve years old, sitting on a low wall, book in hand. The girl was not totally absorbed in her book, apparently, since she took notice of Bea as she went by. "Begging your pardon, Madam, but I don't think I've ever seen that style of dress before. I mean under your cloak. Is that a new style from Europe?"

The girl was quite observant, since the cloak covered almost everything. Bea had not given any thought to how she appeared, but now realized that jeans and a sweatshirt would definitely look out of place. The little girl had just seen her jeans peeking out from under the cloak and found it curious. If she had noticed it, then others would as well. Bea replied, "You are an observant young lady, and yes, this is a new style, but I do not think I like it very much. My name is Beatrisa, and I am a visitor from a faraway land. What is your name?"

"I am Harriet Hanson, and I work in the mill just over there", she said, indicating the Boott Mills building. "Like many girls my age, I'm a doffer. Since you are not from here, I will explain: my job is to pass through the various spinning rooms in the mill, picking up the full bobbins and replacing them with empty ones. It doesn't pay much, but it also isn't such hard work either. And I have plenty of time to improve my mind", she said, glancing down at her book. "We get many visitors here in this city, travelling lecturers and preachers and so on, from many different places. Could you tell me what land you are from?"

"I come from Brazil. Do you know where that is?" The girl nodded, seeming a little bit insulted at such a question. "Our Emperor has sent a delegation here to study your remarkable industrial experiment. This is my first day here, and I am taking a walk around the city." This was something that Bea had remembered from school: she knew that a few years from now, the Brazilian Emperor Dom Pedro would actually visit Lowell, one of many dignitaries who came to see the world-famous mill complexes.

The girl seemed to accept all of this, and replied, "I am sure you will enjoy it. I would just advise you not to wander over in that direction", indicating the paddy camps to the west, "since it is not a safe place for an unaccompanied woman to pass, particularly at night."

"Paddy camps? What does that mean?"

"That is where the Irish laborers live. A lot of the people here think the Irish are nothing but trouble. They drink too much, and they start a lot of fights. My mother thinks that the Irish should all be sent away, that they should not even be considered human beings. But I think that the ones who cause so much trouble, it's not because they're Irish, it's because they are poor. Certainly a lot of poor people who aren't Irish don't behave any better. And the Irish who live up on Chapel Hill seem perfectly respectable".

Bea's mind was buzzing with several impressions at once. She had a growing sense that the Irish of this time might have something in common with the Brazilians of her time, and she very much wanted to see what her own neighborhood on Chapel Hill looked like. Also, there was something about the little girl that struck a chord in her memory. It was the name! Harriet Hanson, after she grew up and got married, would one day write a famous book about her experiences in the mills. A book which Bea had read in school! No wonder the girl seemed so perceptive.

Bea also realized that she should probably make herself a little less conspicuous. After taking her leave of Harriet, she found a quiet alley and rolled up the legs of her jeans so that they wouldn't show beneath her cloak.

Finding her way about the city was quite easy, since the streets were laid out almost exactly as she knew them. Many of the buildings were familiar, as well. Bea made her way along Merrimack Street, up Central Street, then turned down the small side street where she lived. She was surprised to see her house right where it always was, then thought it was silly for her to be surprised. She knew the house was old. In her time, the house was divided into apartments, and she lived with her mother and Carolina on the first floor. In this time, it looked like the house was probably occupied by one family.

She must have been standing there on the street for a while, when a jolly voice rang out from the front window, "Faith, girl! If you don't present a puzzle! Are you lost, or are you looking at ghosts? Either way, why don't you come in and have some tea?"

Bea was actually at a loss for words. She just couldn't think of a reasonable story to justify her presence here. This was her home, but then again it wasn't. These were probably the first people ever to live in this house. What was she doing here? She truthfully didn't know. As fascinating and incredible as this abrupt visit to the past was, she couldn't see how it was going to help Carolina. Or anybody.

As the front door opened, Bea saw a middle-aged woman with a round, beaming face excitedly gesturing for her to come in. She meekly complied, trying to keep a grip on her feelings as she walked through her own living room, into her own kitchen, and sat down. The furniture was all different, of course, and the walls were a different color. And the lady of the house was being energetically hospitable. "Have a seat, dear, the tea is almost ready. And here, have some cake with it. Just made it. Now, my girl, I hope that you speak English. To my eyes, you look like an Indian, but I confess I have never seen one with my own eyes. Oh, forgive my rudeness, what am I thinking? My name is Margaret Conlon, and my husband David runs a dry goods store on Merrimack Street. I would be there now, but business is slow this time of morning, and goodness knows there's always cleaning to be done here."

Bea was starting to feel comfortable in spite of herself. She wanted to offer as much of the truth as possible. She said "I am very pleased to meet you. My name is Beatrisa. I am not an Indian, but from Brazil. And I was looking at your house because it looks very much like my own."

"Well, I never! Brazil! Such a long way! And what a coincidence! Well, we are very happy with this house, we just built it two years ago. About time, too. The Camps are no place to raise little ones. But Beatrisa dear, are you lost? This is an odd part of the city for a young woman to be walking around in alone. Not dangerous, mind you, just odd."

"No, thank you for your concern, I'm not lost, just taking some time to learn about the city before my group leaves for Boston."

Bea's hostess took this in with a slightly skeptical look, but did not break her cheerful mood. "Well that's fine. I'm sorry if I seem nosy, it's just so exciting to see someone as… unusual as you, and I hope I don't offend."

"No, absolutely not. I appreciate your concern. And your tea and cake are wonderful." This was sincere. Mrs. Conlon's tea and cake really were wonderful, the most reassuring sensation that Bea had experienced in the past 24 hours.

Feeling so at ease, Bea was able to ask a question that had been weighing on her mind since her chat with little Harriet Hanson. "Mrs. Conlon, I desperately hope you are not offended by this, but I am curious about one thing. The Irish down in the camps, they are very poor, and the established people, the Yankees, they seem to look down on the Irish and won't allow them to be citizens, with all the rights that Americans are supposed to have. Yet you seem very optimistic. What do you see in your future?"

Mrs. Conlon paused for a moment before answering. "Well, my dear, I am not offended. You are from a far off land, and you wouldn't necessarily know how things are. My people, in Ireland, have been under the heel of the English for centuries. Believe me, even at its worst, the situation here is much better. But I know what you mean: as hard as we work it seems that we will never really be accepted as Americans. But you shouldn't take appearances to heart. People will say what they say, and do what they do, but they aren't the whole world. The future is everyone's to make. And while the Irish seem to be fighting amongst themselves all the time, most of the time we're actually helping each other. And we're all working hard to build a future, one that will belong to us. All of us are doing this, including the ones in the Camps. The time will come when the Americans will see what we have built, and what we have made of ourselves, and will realize that they need to be a part of it at least as much as we need to be a part of their society. After all, we didn't come all this way to just give up: we could have done that back home much more conveniently!"

This was so encouraging to Bea that she had to fight the impulse to tell Mrs. Conlon how right she had turned out to be.

Realizing that she needed to head back to meet with Tin and O'Malley, she made her thanks and apologies and prepared to leave. Mrs. Conlon had a parting word with her at the door:

"My dear, I sense that there is much that you are holding back, that you weren't telling me the whole truth about who you are and why you're here. But my old grandmother in County Cork used to say I have the second sight: I am hardly ever wrong about people. Young lady, I believe that what you are doing here is good, important, and difficult, but that you have the strength and courage to carry it through."

Bea replied in a small, sad voice, looking down at her feet, "Then you know more than I do…"

Undeterred, the lady continued, "Be of good cheer, girl. I will pray for you. God watches over all of us, but I am sure He will keep a special watch on you."

"Thank you, Mrs. Conlon. That means a lot to me. You go with God as well. Good bye".

Bea barely noticed her surroundings as she made her way back to the street where she had earlier parted company with the others. Tin was waiting patiently, and seemed quite glad to see her. "Did you enjoy your wanderings, Beatrisa?" he asked. "Yes", she said, "it was actually very illuminating. But I am still quite mystified about how we got here, and I am still anxious to find out how this will help me find my sister".

At this point, Professor O'Malley came into view, striding briskly down Lowell Street. He seemed to be in good humor, in spite of a gash above his left eye which was bleeding quite a bit. "I've had a fascinating time seeing the water power system in action, and how they are extending the canals. It's a unique opportunity". Then noticing that Bea and Tin were staring with alarm at his forehead, he said "Oh, that. While I was taking a look at the Western Canal, I inadvertently got in the way of a little disagreement between some Cork men and some Connaught men. This disagreement took the form of flying bricks, so it was evidently the wrong place for bystanders. Don't worry, it probably looks worse than it feels. If either of you has a handkerchief, I would appreciate the use of it."

Tin was apparently waiting for something else, and moments later it arrived: a carriage pulled by a pair of fine-looking black horses, and driven by a distinguished-looking white-haired man. Tin once again led the conversation. "Beatrisa, and Professor O'Malley, this is Charles Healey. He will be accompanying us on our way to an important conference. Mr. Healey already knows who you are." Healey gave the two of them a polite tip of the hat, while concentrating on the horses. O'Malley chimed in excitedly, "And I certainly know who he is, he is the one who organized the Irish laborers who built all of this. He is a very famous figure in the history of the city." For his part, Charles Healey seemed to be avoiding eye contact with Bea and O'Malley, and did not speak at first. They all piled into the carriage, and Tin told them, "We are taking a ride to an island located a few miles upriver in

Tyngsborough. It so happens that we must cross the river to get there, so we are heading for the bridge at the end of Central Street. It should be quite safe to cross there."

This piqued Bea's interest. There's that thing about where to cross the river, she thought, but didn't have an opportunity to speak up just yet, as Tin continued, "This ride will take about an hour, and in this time I will let you know, at last, what this is all about, and I will attempt to answer any questions you may have." With Charles Healey at the reins, they made their way a short distance east along the narrow street, crossed the river, then headed west again, to yet another strange destination.

Chapter 9
A Visit with Passaconaway

The long ride provided the opportunity for some explanations, and Tin told Beatrisa and O'Malley about the Firsts, the Demon and its imprisonment behind the Falls, and about the Seconds and why they were brought forth upon the world. Though O'Malley had perceived the existence of the Firsts in his experience with the Sight, much of this was as new to him as it was to Beatrisa. He grew excited at hearing about the Seconds and how they dealt with humans. "That actually explains a great deal" he said, "There are so many arbitrary social conventions that we have inherited from the Sumerians, conventions that have persisted for thousands of years for no obvious reason and now are the norm around the world. Particularly in the demarcation of time. I mean, dividing the day into 24 hours, organizing work around a seven day week, and so on. These seem quite arbitrary, and there is no reason why these and not other conventions were adopted. But if they were part of the accommodation of agricultural life to the world of the Firsts, then there would be a reason for this persistence."

Beatrisa spoke up. "You have still told us very little about what sort of person you are, Tin."

Tin replied, "My apologies. We are actually very similar to humans, except for some subtle genetic manipulation, courtesy of the Seconds. While they do their work mainly by influencing humans in dreams and visions, occasionally they require concrete action in the physical realm, and that is what folks like me are for. There are not many of us: perhaps as many as thirty in the entire world." At this, Healey grumbled under his breath. Tin responded, "And yet, we have acquired a sinister reputation in the folklore of many different peoples. This is not entirely our fault. True, we tend to be rather direct and single-minded in the pursuance of our missions, and unfortunately our actions can often be frightening to humans. But these missions are provided by the Seconds, our immediate masters, who do not always agree with one another. Their reason for existence revolves around you humans, and the need to minimize the problems that you pose for the Firsts and the orderly existence of earthly life. Some Seconds, as I told you, have chosen to guide humans along a harmonious path. Others feel that the answer is to altogether eliminate the practice of agriculture and force all humans to return to a herding life. You can imagine the consequences in the short term."

"Yes", O'Malley replied, "Herding can only support a tiny fraction of the world's present population. This would be genocide on an unimaginable scale!"

"And I find the long term consequences troubling as well", said Tin. "Perhaps the remaining humans would lead a better, more sustainable existence, in harmony with the rest of the community of life. But what measures must be taken to insure that no one in the future has the urge to till the soil, acts on that urge, and rediscovers the benefits of doing so? This feels like a very unwholesome restriction of the potential of your species, and as much as you may seem like a plague upon the Earth, I do not think that the Firsts would have made possible the existence of beings such as yourselves without a serious purpose. And although this remains an ongoing debate among the Seconds, fortunately the majority opinion is still in favor of the methods chosen 10,000 years ago."

"As for me, my current 'mentor' among the Seconds is the one the Bashaba calls Wamesit, whose home is the woods and hills watered by Hale's Brook, just to the south in Chelmsford and Carlisle. Wamesit is probably alone among the Seconds in Its knowledge of the Demon and the danger it poses, and is also aware of some unique tools that we have available to defeat it. Perhaps the greatest of these is the connection which allowed us to move between this time and yours."

As long as Tin was explaining things, Bea thought that this was a good time to mention something that had been on her mind for a while. "You have mentioned, twice, that we should only cross the river below the falls, not above. I can understand this, if there is some dangerous creature in the water. That also explains why that awful cult leader was able to walk on water. It didn't look like a trick. But the strange thing is, my boss at the computer shop made me promise the same thing about the bridges. Does everybody except me know about this demon?"

Tin looked really surprised for once, and stopped to think. "Your boss? I knew there was another Talent in the city, but it eluded me. Tell me about him."

Bea said, "There's not that much to tell. His name is Rudy Foster, he came here from Jamaica about ten years ago, and he runs a used-PC store in the Highlands."

Charles Healey spoke up for the first time since the ride began. "Jamaica? Foster? My sister just married a man named Foster, and they moved to Jamaica to manage a plantation. I might have known. Nothing but coincidences lately. I feel like a marionette on strings." With that, he fell back into a grumpy silence.

O'Malley quickly broke the silence with more questions. "Concerning this time travel that we just experienced. How exactly does that work?"

Tin replied, "In spite of my deep misgivings regarding the action itself, I find the mechanism quite interesting. I believe that the scientists of your time have been seriously considering the existence of additional spatial dimensions beyond the familiar three. There is at least one, which can be quite useful, although its full extent is but a quarter-inch. In order to effect the passage between your time and this, powers beyond my ken have applied a bend to the universe, so that the two times are close enough to touch one another within the breadth of this dimension. It requires a special sort of manipulation to make use of this dimension. I will show you."

Tin pulled off both of his leather gloves and held up the right-hand one. "Observe my right glove. I can move it up and down and sideways, and rotate it every which way, but there is no way I can turn it to make it identical in shape to my left glove. That is, without turning it inside out. And the inside looks different from the outside, so that wouldn't work either."

"That sounds reasonable so far." said O'Malley, watching closely, as though he was expecting a trick of some sort.

"Watch as I apply a rotation of an altogether different kind", said Tin, and, holding the right glove in his fist, extended his arm out. His hand appeared to fade a little, to lose color and turn grey and out of focus. The outstretched hand then executed a few quick motions which were difficult to follow. Tin drew his hand back, opened his fist, and held the gloves against each other. Now they were both obviously left-hand gloves. However, one of them had the same wear marks that the right-hand glove had had, but reversed.

O'Malley did not know quite how to react to this at first, and it was not immediately obvious to him how this related to the question at hand. So he just looked at Tin, with his attention divided as he thought about all the other uncanny things that he had just seen.

Bea's reaction was different. In an uncharacteristic outburst, she shouted, "*DO THAT AGAIN*!" Seeing what Tin had just done with the glove, she was overwhelmed with a feeling that this was something of profound importance to her, personally. Tin repeated the procedure, the glove in the fist, the reaching, the fading, the drawing back, and this time it was once again a right-hand glove. Bea was not the least bit skeptical that Tin had done what he appeared to have done.

Tin was not about to let the import of this demonstration be lost on O'Malley. "May I borrow your watch for a moment, Professor?" O'Malley handed it over, a bit puzzled. Tin reached out with it, and drew it back, as before with the glove. The watch face now had all the numbers reversed, as if seen in a mirror, and the second hand was sweeping counter-clockwise. What struck O'Malley was that the inscription on the back of the watch, a warm testimonial from some members of the Physics department at MIT, had also been reversed. How ironic, he thought. Tin restored the watch to its original condition and returned it to O'Malley. For a while Tin and O'Malley talked about dimensions, forces and particles, but Bea became completely withdrawn, and did not speak, or take much note of her surroundings, for the remainder of the ride, for this trick with the glove had made a deep impression on her.

At length the carriage arrived at a quiet place near the river in Tyngsborough, far from any farms or any other signs of human activity. A narrow dirt trail led from the main road toward the river, and they began walking along it. Tin explained, "You may be surprised at who you are about to meet. He is probably the most knowledgeable person on the subject of the Demon, on this continent or any other. He is Passaconaway, and was the Bashaba, or Emperor, of all the Indian nations of New England at the time of the first English settlements."

O'Malley objected, "Have we time-traveled again without knowing it? I agree that we must be near Passaconaway's final home, but he died in 1665!"

Now Charles Healey spoke up. "There are documents in Boston that state that Passaconaway was granted an island in this location by the Massachusetts General Court, and retired here in 1662 after making his farewell speech on the banks of the Merrimack. There is no report in the state archives of any further contact with him, so it is simply assumed that he died shortly thereafter. But the natives have a few stories that did not make it into the Yankee archives."

O'Malley considered this. "He had quite an amazing reputation in his time. It was said that he was a great conjurer, that he could make lakes burn, trees dance and rocks flow like water. And some legends state that he made an appearance in northern New Hampshire long after the date of his supposed death. And they describe him ascending into heaven, as well! I always assumed that someone was just borrowing stories from the New Testament, and inserting more familiar people and places."

"But the big mystery about him, at least from his people's viewpoint, was why, with all his powers, he permitted the Europeans to settle in New England at all."

Bea had also heard of Passaconaway, but was not so clear on the details of his life as everyone else seemed to be. Other than what little she had heard of him in school, all she knew of Passaconaway was a rather sad-looking little stone monument by the river, across the street from a McDonalds, a stone so small and inconspicuous that it was usually hidden by the weeds surrounding it. On the other hand, one of the peaks in the White Mountains was named after him, so perhaps in a different context, farther from the banks of the Merrimack River, he was nearly on a par with George Washington, after whom the very highest peak was named.

They had reached what appeared to be the end of the trail, at the edge of a little weed-choked marsh alongside the river. But Healey took the lead, and boldly stepped out onto the marsh, and suddenly the place where he stepped was not a part of the marsh but a dirt causeway, leading to an island which hadn't been there a moment ago. Following Healey, they all stepped across the causeway, onto the island, and made their way along a trail leading up to the top of a small hill. As soon as they stepped onto the island, the weather suddenly changed: there were no more clouds in the sky, and it felt like a very pleasant day in June, no longer a gloomy overcast March day.

As they walked along the path, they passed a vegetable garden and a fish weir, and a frame where some fish were being dried in the sun. At the top of the hill they saw a small log house with a wooden placard above the entrance. The placard was carved with a stylized drawing of a bear. O'Malley recognized it. "That's Passaconaway's symbol. His name literally means, Son of the Bear."

A tall man with long grey hair walked out of the entrance as they approached. He was dressed in a long, loose white robe, almost like a hippie guru of the 1960s. Beatrisa was suddenly reminded of the ridiculous appearance of Oswald in his robes, performing his "ceremony". But Passaconaway did not look at all ridiculous: in a similar outfit, he looked in fact every bit as impressive as Oswald had tried and failed to look. Looking at this man, it was easy for Bea to picture him as the Emperor that her traveling companions claimed that he had been.

He greeted them warmly, in fluent, albeit old-fashioned, English, and invited them to sit. As they sat outdoors, on benches made from split logs, he served them tea in exquisite china cups, which must have been fantastically expensive in his time. The tea was excellent, and they all relaxed as Passaconaway spoke:

"My friends, we have the weight of a crisis upon us, which some of you know and some of you are just beginning to learn. My life story is bound up in this peril, so that is where I will begin.

"I was born to royalty, and spent much of my youth learning the skills that a leader of my people must have. However, this left considerable time for idleness, and I would spend many days alone, exploring the region of the Musketahquid [the Concord River]. It was during these wanderings that Wamesit first spoke to me. This was in the headwaters of the flow that you may know as Hale's Brook, or Rivermeadow. Many days I spent in conversation with this God, learning the ways of the earth and the spirits. Those born into ruling families learn a type of conjuring as a normal part of their education, for it can be a useful tool for inspiring awe and obedience in one's subjects, and fear in one's enemies. But from Wamesit, I learned a deeper magic that was more than trickery: It showed me how to mold and change the essential fabric of the world. I was young, and did not know that this knowledge was not commonplace, so I was not shy about practicing it, and thus gained an early reputation as a great conjurer.

"This gift of power brought with it a terrible responsibility. When my father passed away, and I took the mantle of empire, despite the many distractions of leadership I became aware of a poison in the heart of my realm. The fishing grounds of the

Meroack, the falls where my people gathered to catch salmon each spring, had a sinister reputation. Between the falls and the sea, all was well. But no one would attempt to farm or maintain a settlement on the upper side of the falls for very long. The outcome was always the same: a few individuals were afflicted with a madness which either took their lives immediately through an act of violence upon themselves, or took many lives as this madness turned outward. In many cases, the afflicted person died mindlessly digging the dirt with his bleeding fingers, as if he could dig a new riverbed by himself.

"The salmon were plentiful at the falls, but it was dangerous to be that close, and settlements were usually short-lived. For my people's safety, a simple warning was sufficient, but I needed to know the cause of this blight. Turning to the mentor of my youth, Wamesit, I received a startling answer. The river is inhabited by a Demon, I was told, the most terrible and dangerous Demon ever brought forth on this Earth. This place, in the river above the falls, in the center of my realm, is its prison. It is the 'Great Unraveler', which unravels the pattern and design of all things that are alive. It is the most dangerous creature imaginable, Wamesit told me, because Its driving need was to kill life of all kinds, including the Gods themselves, and once that was done, It would kill Itself. Then the Earth would be left a barren rock, incapable of bearing life, unto the end of time.

"I had been granted the ability to see and understand much that is hidden, and I eventually found the opportunity to observe the Demon directly. I could clearly see Its lurking menace, and felt Its fury, but was not harmed by It. I also understood the form that the madness sometimes took, because the digging always took place in a small brook which flowed into the river just above the falls. It would not take a great deal of digging to connect this brook, through a small marsh, to the Musketahquid, thus permitting the Demon to flow out with the water and wreak Its mad destruction upon the world.

"The coming of the Europeans was therefore very bad news indeed. The fact that they brought filth and disease, the destruction of our hunting grounds, and a barbaric habit of casual thievery cloaked in an insincere, shallow mockery of law and piety, this we would learn in due course. What I knew immediately was that these people were diggers of the earth, who would make short work of the Demon's escape, should they be brought under Its influence.

"As is well known, in my first contact with the Europeans at Plymouth, I attempted to persuade them to leave. According to your people's history, I was trying to frighten them back to the sea with a display of my power. This was a childish misinterpretation on their part: if I had intended this, they would have been suitably terrified, I can assure you. Rather, I was simply attempting to communicate with them. I assumed that people with the powers that they appeared to have were in communication with the same sort of Gods that I knew, and I tried to explain to them the danger that lay in wait at Meroack and warned them to avoid that place. Sadly, although they flattered themselves as people uniquely close to the Gods, it became clear that they were ignorant, and had not been granted the same privilege of communication that I had. In retrospect, I realize that I erred by showing them respect in this instance, and it would have been wiser to fill their sky with flying orange snakes, turn their clothing to masses of biting worms, and send them running back to their boats and on to Virginia. But in the long run it would have changed nothing. I have had a growing suspicion that it was the Demon who lured these people here in the first place. Its influence is overwhelming in close contact, but can still be felt at a tremendous distance, and its ways are subtle.

"As more and more Europeans arrived and made their farms ever closer to the Demon's domain, a drastic change in my priorities was required. With special knowledge came a special duty, and this duty was not only to my people, but to all life, since I could clearly see the danger. There were simply too many Europeans, and the effectiveness of conjuring is greatly diminished when very large numbers of people are involved. They could not be sent away, so their activities in the area of the falls had to be closely watched, and guided if necessary. What they did elsewhere was of little importance compared to this. In order to gain time, I passed the leadership of my people to my son Wannalancit, and impressed upon him the need to keep the Europeans away for a time. This is the reason why he accepted the teaching of a Christian minister, John Eliot, and established a community of what the Europeans called 'praying Indians' to prevent the farmers of Chelmsford from settling there. This was successful, though the advantage was only temporary: the village dwindled, through sicknesses brought both by the Demon and by the Europeans, and by the war between races which flared up shortly afterward.

"History records that I was granted an island by the Massachusetts General Court, to which I retired, and presumably died. What history does not record is that, on my island, I removed myself from the flow of time, the better to study the Demon and maintain a vigil, so that when the need arose, I could take such action as needed, and enlist the aid of whatever wise people could be found. Thus, though centuries have passed, I have maintained my vigil, and know the ways of the Demon as well as any human can.

"Know this: the time is upon you! Mister Healey, I see that you have brought visitors from a time yet to come, as requested. The Gods made this passage possible because this crisis binds these two times together. The digging of the canal in the Vale of Madness was an event that I had been dreading all these years.

"I also believe that there is one of your kind", indicating Tin, "presently in the service of the Demon, and that in the year from which your guests have come, this one is still active."

Charles Healey answered, "That would explain much of what has happened of late. I have recently been maneuvered out of my position of authority over the maintenance of the canals by the machinations of someone whom I have never seen, and not for lack of trying. But this is monstrous! These creatures are tireless, cunning and utterly ruthless. Begging your pardon", this with a grudging nod toward Tin.

Passaconaway answered, "That may be so. However, if one of this kind is in the Demon's service, it must mean that he is damaged in some way. This may limit his capability somewhat."

O'Malley could not hold himself back at this point. "Bashaba, if there is an elf who is helping the Demon to escape in our time, and life still exists in that year, then how can there be a crisis now, in 1842? Doesn't that mean that any attempt to release the monster in this time must have failed?"

Passaconaway paused, at a loss for a moment as to how to explain himself. "The Old Ones are exceedingly thrifty with information. What they do not tell, we must infer. I know very clearly that the danger exists in both times, that these dangers are connected, and must be dealt with in both times. The Gods have brought about this time passage, an exceptional event, because whatever action is required, must be done by you, and it must have its effect both in this time and in your time. They are relying on humans to undo danger that has been wrought by the actions of humans."

He focused on each of them in turn. "Mister Healey, you have done your duty marvelously well, and after this battle, you may rest from your labors. You are correct in assuming that your authority over the canals has been usurped by this servant of the

Demon. It is good that you saved some of the stone from your homeland: you will have need of it soon.

"Young Tin, it comforts me that one of your kind is assisting in this struggle. I am confident that you can withstand the influence of the evil one. You must concentrate your attention on the one who failed, for he will be at the center of the Demon's plan of escape. He can act in the world of humans with a dexterity that the Demon does not possess.

"Teacher O'Malley, you have been granted the ability to See, as I have. I was fortunate to inherit a strong constitution, and my body was hardened by a vigorous outdoor life, and even so the use of the Sight came close to killing me at times. You will need to use the Sight soon in this struggle, but you can turn it to other purposes if the outcome is successful. You will need to strengthen your body, however, if you wish to have the full advantage of it."

Passaconaway's last words were for Bea. "Young woman, you are the one whom I was most anxious to meet. I was hoping that you were the Warrior who is needed for what is to come, the one who can take my place, and go further than I was able. I see that Tin chose correctly."

Beatrisa had had just about all that she going to tolerate. She had heard some interesting things, and seen some interesting things, that might be important in some scholarly or abstract sense, but it seemed as though the day was wasted. By this point, she could have searched the city on foot, found Carolina and dragged her home. This extravagant but pointless flattery meant nothing, as far as she could see. She began to turn away in frustration from the tall man in the robes.

Passaconaway's tone became sharper and more urgent. "Young woman, I know that you have other concerns, but I must have your full attention. I have much to tell you, and precious little time." He reached out his hand, and gently touched Beatrisa on her forehead with his outstretched finger. The effect was like turning on a light in a dark room, a room which Bea had always assumed to be an empty closet, but which was revealed by the light to be a huge storeroom filled with treasures. In an instant, she clearly understood everything that she had seen and heard this day, and much more besides. It seemed to her that she had always known, but had never chosen to pay attention. And there were so many powerful tools available to her, things which had always been there for her to use, it seemed. The challenge was to sort out what these abilities were, and how best to use them.

She also understood the obligation that came with this understanding and power. The Demon in the river, and the fate of the Earth and all that lived upon it, were her personal concern, because she was uniquely able to do something about them. She tried to stammer out an answer, an apology of sorts, to the Bashaba, but he stopped her.

"Go now, Warrior, and prepare. I wish you success for all our sakes. This battle is yours now, and you must be ready. But the time will come when you see that it is not the end but the beginning. Then, we will talk again."

With the discussion at an end, and their tea finished, the guests prepared to head back down the path and off the island. As he bade them farewell, Passaconaway offered one final, apparently idle thought: "It is truly unfortunate that there are not two of these creatures, for they would surely destroy each other". They stepped off the causeway and onto the bank, and the island disappeared from view as if it had never been. They started their carriage journey back to Lowell, discussing what they had learned. All except Beatrisa, who was still silent, lost in thought.

The return to the present was brisk. They alit from the carriage in front of the Boott Mills, they bade farewell to Charles Healey, and Tin brought them back through the mysterious doorway in the basement through which they had made their passage before. This time, however, Bea paid very close attention to everything that Tin did as he led them through the time passage. Walking back upstairs they found themselves back in the familiar surroundings of Lowell as they knew it.

Chapter 10

In which Beatrisa Turns a Clock Backward

Beatrisa, O'Malley and Tin walked along the sidewalk, trying to assimilate everything that they had just seen and heard. Bea and O'Malley felt a bit stunned. Tin was distressed at the realization that, from this point on, he, along with everyone else, was totally dependent on what these two would be able to do. Bea was the first to speak. "We need to talk this over for a while. And I think that the PC shop would be a good place." Tin agreed. "Yes, and I want to talk with your boss. You said that he asked you not to cross the river upstream of the falls. I would like to know how he knows this."

Now it was Bea's turn to lead the way. It was now late in the afternoon, the daylight was fading, and the weather was just as unpleasant as it had been the previous day. But the group barely noticed the cold now. They took the walkway along the Merrimack Canal past the high school and St. Anne's, went past the National Park Visitors' Center and the Swamp Locks, up the hill to the overpass, and down a short stretch of Middlesex Street to the small block of stores where the PC shop was located. It was near closing time, but the door was unlocked, and Rudy was behind the counter. As soon as Rudy saw Bea enter the shop with the others, he rushed to the door, locked it, closed the blinds and flipped over the "Closed" sign. He stared at Tin in apprehension. "You are....I have seen another like you. Bea, who is this creature?"

Tin, for his part, was equally amazed. This man could see through Tin's concealment! And Tin had noticed a number of cleverly camouflaged hexes hung about the doorway and at various places within the shop. Bea's boss knew a thing or two about concealment himself, and had gone to a great deal of trouble to protect... who? Himself? Bea? Both? Clearly he know something about the Demon, but how much did he know?

Bea sensed the tension, and tried to defuse the situation. "Rudy, this is Tin, and I guess you can see that he's a little bit different from us. Is that what you mean? That you have seen another one like him? I swear, he's OK, Carolina is in trouble and he's shown me what I can do to help her".

Tin spoke up at last. "Mr. Foster, you surprise me. I'll wager Beatrisa has no idea what a fortress you have made of this little shop. I assume that this is for her protection. She has exceptional capabilities, and I will assume further that you are aware of this. I have been searching this city for allies in a battle against a great evil. I sensed your presence but you eluded me, despite how close you were to Beatrisa. Might I ask: who are you, and how does it happen that you know these things?"

Rudy relaxed: like a punctured balloon, he relaxed. He quietly slipped a fistful of dried leaves back into a drawer behind the counter. He had been told that this variety of leaf was an effective weapon against beings like this, but he was just as glad not to put this to the test. Mostly, Rudy felt an overwhelming sense of relief, that Beatrisa was becoming engaged in the struggle for which she was destined, that there were others who could show her what she needed to know, and that, very likely, his lifelong role as her protector was reaching a successful conclusion.

No longer needing to conceal his mission, he explained to Tin, and to Beatrisa and O'Malley as well, about his family's business, and about the vision which had shaped his life. As he spoke, Beatrisa gave him some strange looks, as though she was unsure whether to be grateful or angry. Either way, she was still too preoccupied to make an issue of it. This was yet another confirmation of the collection of ridiculous, but true, things that she had been told over the past two days. And now she knew a few things which the others did not.

Tin and O'Malley exchanged what they knew of the Demon with Rudy, and told him about their recent visit to the Lowell of 1842, and their discussion with Passaconaway. From Passaconaway, they had come away with the understanding that the battle must be joined in both years in parallel, and that there was very likely a Third working on the Demon's behalf. At this, Rudy spoke up excitedly.

"I have something to contribute, folks, concerning that dangerous fellow. I was in his office last night, in City Hall. I was afraid for my life, since I am sure that I was not supposed to be able to see his true appearance. But since I was delivering a new computer, I took the opportunity to install a surveillance program. We can watch everything he does on that computer from here, and I do not believe that we can be detected."

Tin was excited at this news. "That explains a great deal. He is entrenched, probably never leaves the building, and must have concealment spells all over the place. You were in great danger, Mr. Foster, as you suspected. But now that we know where he is to be found, can you show us some of this surveillance?"

Rudy led them to his office, and opened up a window on his computer screen which showed the accumulated data so far. "See there? He's been placing more orders for explosives, and checking the work schedules for all the police and fire stations in the city"

"An excellent beginning", said Tin. "Now, my dear Professor, I think it is time that you use that Sight of yours to try and make sense of this new information, if you are up to it. Please examine the information we see here, and try and relate it to what we know of the Third in City Hall, and of the Father Oswald cult."

O'Malley nodded, and took on a glazed expression for several long minutes. He stared at Rudy's computer screen at first, then walked to the front of the shop and stared out at the street for a longer time. Walking back to Rudy's office, he collapsed in a chair and shook his head. "I am beginning to see. I think I may know what they are going to do" he said, wiping the sweat from his face with a handkerchief.

Bea had watched this procedure patiently, but at this point offered what seemed to be a change in subject. "Wasn't there a big flood in Lowell in 1842? A couple of months after the time of our visit, I mean."

Tin scowled angrily, and looked as though he might rush out, but controlled his anger. No need to ask: Bea and O'Malley already knew how much every aspect of time travel offended Tin, and he would certainly find foreknowledge of events in his own time offensive. But O'Malley was excited about this. "That's it! That explains all the things I saw in the canal system in 1842 that looked wrong. The locks appeared weak, the stone linings were missing many blocks, a lot of silt had accumulated everywhere. It went beyond neglect, it was as though someone was sabotaging the canal. It would make sense in advance of a major flood. And I'll bet it was that same nasty old leprechaun doing it!"

Tin had been getting plenty of practice at holding his temper lately, so he let that last comment pass by. Actually, this was new, and useful: look for the one in a position to openly damage the canal with impunity. And especially look for signs of concealment spells associated with such activity. Even if we can't see him, his actions leave a trail that we can follow!

The discussion turned to speculation about Father Oswald and how he might be connected with the plot. Although this should have been the subject of greatest interest to Bea, she sat silent once again, wrapped up in her own thoughts.

Finally, Tin changed the subject. "Assuming we are able to find out exactly when, where and how this Third will make his move, what can we do to stop him?"

The silence didn't last long. Bea quietly said, "I have a couple of ideas. It will take some practice to turn this into something useful, but I saw what you did, and I saw how Passaconaway's island was set up, so I thought I could put some of the same principles to work. Watch this for a minute…"

Bea did several things as the rest of them watched. First, she appeared to flicker in and out of view, slowly at first and then faster. Then, she stretched out her hand, and a glowing ball of yellow light appeared, floating above her palm. She gave the ball a gentle push, and it floated slowly across the room towards the clock on Rudy's office wall. It was a novelty clock, with a picture of Daffy Duck on the face. Daffy was forever staring at the numeral "2" as his arms swiveled around to mark the hours and minutes. As the glowing ball reached the clock, it appeared to splash against it and disappear. There was a slight snapping sound, and all of a sudden the clock face was reversed. Daffy was still staring at the numeral "2", but now he was facing left, and the "2" was backward.

Bea produced another ball of light in her hand, and sent it sailing over to the clock again. This time, the splash brought the clock face back to normal. Daffy seemed unperturbed, and Rudy, Tin and O'Malley were delighted. They knew they had just seen something uncanny, and they were prepared to believe that this was relevant to the task of battling a demon, if only because Bea seemed to think so herself. Actually, Bea had not been completely forthcoming with the others. It was not simply clues gained from watching what Tin and Passaconaway did: the Bashaba had made Beatrisa aware of an incredible variety of methods for manipulating space and time. The challenge now was to figure out exactly which ones to use for which purpose.

Although there was clearly more to be discussed, Bea hastily took her leave. "Excuse me, gentlemen," she said, "but let us not forget that my little sister is in danger, and I must rescue her before I can think about saving the rest of the world. You can stay here, if Rudy doesn't mind," (Rudy nodded agreement) "and I will be back in an hour or two, so we can finish making our plans."

A short while later, as the shadows grew long with the approach of sunset, Bea was walking up Mansur Street in Lowell's Outer Belvidere neighborhood. This steep hill overlooking the downtown area was where, in the 19th century, the mill agents and other high and mighty folks had built their mansions. Most of the mansions were still here, though some were occupied by businesses or other institutions, and others had been divided into apartments. Bea was breathing heavily from the steep climb from the bridge over the Concord River up to this neighborhood. She had one particular institution in mind, and now knew which one of these mansions it occupied.

A small, discreet yet somehow gross and tasteless sign at the front gate announced this particular mansion as the home of the Church of the Divine Spirit. As Bea drew near, she thought it looked more like a frat house than a church, with slovenly college-aged kids and young adults lounging on the front porch. Perhaps they were there to challenge intruders, but this was irrelevant, since no ordinary humans would have been able to focus on Beatrisa for more than a fraction of a second. It was a simple enough trick, phasing in and out rapidly, and it seemed to adequately confuse these would-be security guards.

Climbing the steps of the front porch and entering the foyer, the frat-house impression was only reinforced. Admittedly, there was some kind of lecture going on in one room, and in another a group chant, and in still another a heated philosophical discussion. But the philosophers seemed a bit tipsy, and the hallways and open areas were littered with empty beer bottles and snoozing believers.

Bea dreaded going up the stairs, but up she went. And Gratia Deus, there was Carolina, in yet another room devoted to an earnest discussion of some technical aspect of the hogwash that this wicked bum Oswald had been foisting on these unfortunates. Carolina was off in a corner by herself, looking miserable. The sight of her filled Beatrisa with joy.

Trying out another tool from her new kit, Bea froze time for everyone in the room except herself and Carolina. Carolina noticed right away that everyone else appeared frozen, saw Beatrisa in the doorway, and looked a little nervous, as though she had been caught doing something wrong. Bea rushed over and hugged her, thrilled to find her sister alive and unhurt. She spoke quickly to reassure her: "Don't worry, Lina-Zinha, I'm not mad at you: I know more about this situation than you think. This is a dangerous place for you, but you had no way of knowing. Let's go, let's get out of here. I have lots to tell you about."

Carolina was beside herself with relief and embarrassment. "I'm so sorry, Bea, it seemed so right, so important, but it turned out so badly. You know, the idea about God experiencing every life and all, and then Oswald letting everyone walk on the water?" Carolina seemed to take it for granted that Bea knew about this. "I was so honored when he invited me to come back to this, I don't know, temple? But it's all so wrong. You see these people?" Carolina gestured at the people in the room, frozen in time as they were apparently making profound observations about something or other. "They're so *stupid*! I couldn't believe it. And back here, after the ceremony, Oswald was trying to grope me while he was talking to everybody about God! It was awful. I had a hard time staying out of his way. Thank God he's kept very busy with a lot of administrative stuff, but I know what he'd rather be doing." Carolina shivered. "But I was so scared, you know? I wanted to leave, but they've got those guys, like bodyguards, at all the doors. I didn't think they would let me leave. How did you get in? Was it that trick you just did, freezing everybody?"

Bea just took all this in, appreciating afresh why she loved her little sister so much. As soon as Carolina had run out of breath, she jumped in. "You'll understand in just a moment. Lina, I have an awful lot to tell you, and not much time to do it. So brace yourself." She reached out and touched Carolina on the forehead, just as Passaconaway had done with her, explaining everything that Beatrisa had learned in the past two days. Carolina's reaction was "Whoa….. and all this is for real? I mean, I see that you can do some really cool things all of a sudden. How did this happen? I mean, why you? Don't get me wrong, you're awesome and I've always known that, but how did you get involved in this?"

This actually made Bea stop and think for a minute, and a few other pieces of the puzzle fell into place. She said, "Do you remember that day that Mãe took us for a picnic at Great Brook Farm? You know, the big park with all the trails? Maybe you don't, you were only seven at the time."

Carolina perked up at this. "Sure I remember. That was just after we came to the US. You and I went wandering off on one of the trails beside a pretty brook, and the next thing we knew, a bunch of Americans were all excited about finding us, and said that we had been missing for hours, and brought us back to Mãe, and she was all upset, and we didn't know what the fuss was about. But right after that, you suddenly started to do really well at school, and got interested in computers, and all that."

Bea had just made the same connection, for the first time. What had happened that day? She and Carolina couldn't remember, though Mãe asked them over and over again. Beatrisa realized now that they had wandered to the center of Wamesit's domain, its seat of power. The universe of possibilities, which Passaconaway had revealed to her, had probably been given to her on that day, and without realizing it, she had been steadily realizing this potential ever since. Odd, that her focus should have been on computers first. Why not physics? That was what she was using now, space-time manipulations that had so many interesting uses.

Bea realized something else. It wasn't just her: both she and Carolina had wandered to that place, had had that contact, and had been changed by it. The change was more obvious in Beatrisa, but what was Carolina carrying, unaware, inside that pretty noggin of hers?

"Lina", she said, "I think I understand what happened, and I think we're in this together. There are a lot of things that I find I am suddenly able to do, and it's as if I was always able, but didn't know it, or I didn't want to know. I think you are in the same situation. Think about it for a minute. What really happened to keep him away from you? Was it his busy schedule, or did you do something without realizing it?"

The light dawned on Carolina. "You know, I really wanted him to be gone, and sure enough, off he went. With a reasonable explanation, of course. Beazee, what are we? And what are we supposed to do?" That was certainly a rhetorical question: in that touch on the forehead, Bea had informed her sister about the creature in the river, about the time passage, about the crisis that must be met in two very different times, everything that Bea knew about the situation.

Bea replied, "I know what I am supposed to do, but I'm scared, Lina. That's a powerful, evil mind there in the water, and it will try to do terrible things to me before I can do something to it. This is all so new, and I have to work hard to understand these new abilities. As for you…."

Carolina answered as though the thought had been hers. "Yes, I see. It's not just the big old monster in the river, it's the people helping it. And obviously I've stepped right into the home of the 'useful idiots'. I can stay here, Bea, really, it's OK, I know how to keep myself safe, and I can tell you exactly what they're up to and how it is supposed to help that awful Lock Monster. And nobody will know I'm doing it."

Bea replied, "That would really help, Lina, and now I know that you can take care of yourself, even in this bad place. But what will I tell Mãe? She's not going to be happy about this."

"Here's a news flash, Beazee: Mãe isn't stupid. If you tell her exactly what we know, she'll understand. Trust her, Irmã. Tell her everything."

A few tenths of a second later, Bea was walking back down Mansur Street, back towards Rudy's shop, where he and O'Malley and Tin were no doubt worrying about her and Carolina. Now, relieved, she would be able to talk strategy with them. Just one more thing before she did that. She needed to make a brief stop at home, to talk with her mother.

Chapter 11

In which a God is Sent up the Creek

(1842 AD)

"G'mornin' Mr. Nash"

"G'mornin' Mr. Nash"

"G'mornin' Mr. Nash"

"G'mornin' Mr. Nash"

It was the start of the weekly ritual. Every Sunday, while the mill girls attended church services, the canals were drained for inspection and maintenance. This had been the practice since the mills first began operation.

Moss had arranged a perfect way for the Master to make Its escape. The smaller branch canals that actually supplied the mills held little interest for him. What mattered was that the Pawtucket itself was cleaned out and widened as part of the overall scheme. The next step was to take control of the maintenance operations. Killing that arrogant martinet Boott made it easy. Moss, who was now going by the name Nash, saw his opportunity one day while Boott was driving though the city in his fine carriage. Curiously, there was no one around at the intersection of Lowell Street and Dutton, and no one had any idea what spooked the horses so badly that they panicked and tipped the carriage over, crushing Boott underneath. Nor was anyone around to record the last thing that Boott saw as he took his last breath, which was "Nash" looking down at him, with no concealment spell, a grin of wicked triumph on his wizened face.

What followed had to be done carefully, to avoid arousing suspicion. Healey had been in charge of the crews, and he had connections. He might be hard to kill, and he would probably see through Nash's concealment. So Nash worked behind the scenes, manipulating, intimidating, and bribing, until he had the influence he needed. Soon enough, Healey found that he was no longer in charge of the maintenance crews. Despite his curiosity, Healey never could catch a glimpse of the man who was now running this operation. Once in charge, Nash never went anywhere without his retinue of bodyguards. He employed spies whose job it was to keep track of Healey's whereabouts, so that Nash could stay well clear of him. And Nash had other spies to watch those spies, and still more spies to watch Healey's spies.

Some changes were instituted in the canal maintenance routines once Nash was in charge. For one thing, workers were rotated. No one worked the same area twice in a row, and there were always new crews coming in to replace the experienced hands. And there were some hand-picked crews that were used for jobs that no one was supposed to know about. What they did, week after week, was pry loose perfectly good stones from the canal walls, and replace them with others. Nash was very specific about which stones were to be removed. Other than that, it seemed that Nash took more of a personal interest in the locks which were left over from the old days, when the Pawtucket had been used to transport barges full of logs, than in the power distribution for the mills. Every week, Nash would demand that all the locks and gates along the Pawtucket be opened and closed, and lubricated if anything didn't move easily. The workers thought this was odd: no barges or boats passed through here anymore, so the locks weren't really needed.

The weekly inspection began with a review of the workers, and with Nash picking which b'hoys would be assigned to which section. They were all lined up, eyes downcast, because it was known that Nash could fly into a violent rage if he thought that he was being stared at, particularly by one of the Irish workmen.

Thus began the weekly ritual. But for Nash, today was anything but ordinary. His crews had nearly completed the process of removing those Irish stones, which the Master could not go near, with blocks of innocuous stone from a quarry in western Massachusetts. Everywhere except right at the end, at the Lower Locks. There had been trouble at that spot. Two months ago, the crew had been instructed to remove two of the Irish stones from the canal walls there. At the end of the day, they reported back to him that the work was complete. Nash had gone to check for himself, and the Irish stones had not been moved! Nash called the crew of three men over to the spot, angrily demanding an explanation. The fools thought they were being commended for their fine work: they acted as if they were proud of getting the job done! Enraged, Nash caused one of the men to slowly roast where he stood, in invisible flames. His coworkers could not see the flames or feel the heat, but they could hear the man's skin crackle and pop, when he wasn't screaming, and saw him turn brown, then black, his bones curled up like some ghastly giant cricket. Nash was expecting confessions now, but the other men were full of bewilderment, on their knees pleading for mercy. They honestly thought that they had done the work, and they even remembered doing it. Nash let the rest of them go. The next week, he took a different crew for the same job, with the same result: the work was not done, and the men acted proud for having done it. Nash was starting to realize what was going on, and satisfied his anger this time by merely putting a curse of impotence on all the men.

The week after, Nash had come to watch. As the new crew headed down into the canal bed, a shimmering distortion appeared over the water of the Concord River, just on the other side of the last lock. Most humans would not have been able to see it at all, but Nash knew what it was: the Brook God Wamesit, an unimpressive Second, whose home was Rivermeadow Brook and its tributaries in Carlisle and Chelmsford. It had apparently wandered off somewhat from Its lair to cause Nash some trouble. It had obviously been clouding the minds of the workmen, to prevent them from removing these stones.

Nash could see the crew abruptly stop what they were doing, then gather their tools and climb out of the canal, with happy smiles on their stupid faces. He stomped over to the canal bed, favoring the crew with clouts on the head as he passed them, then grabbed a crowbar and climbed down into the canal bed to do the work himself. To his surprise, though he tried with all his strength, he could not get closer than ten feet from the stones that he wanted to remove, and the crowbar felt so heavy in his hands that he had to drop it. Wamesit could not cloud his mind, but It could still stop him from doing this work.

The project of replacing stones had to cease for a week while Nash studied the matter. He spent as much of his time as possible at the Lower Locks, trying to goad the Second into appearing so that he could study It. Last week he got a lucky break. He was at the Locks and saw the Second emerge into the Concord River from Rivermeadow Brook, and start moving down the river. But, for some reason, some mill engineers were dumping dye waste into the Concord today. Normally this sort of waste went right into the Merrimack, but this load must have come from one of the mills closer to this spot. The surprising thing was that the Second seemed to be held back by the dye: It would not approach the contaminated water. Nash formed a hypothesis, and set up an experiment to test it.

Today, the crew was sent, like the previous ones, into the canal bed to pry loose some Irish stones from the canal wall. The men dutifully climbed down with their tools. As expected, the shimmering appeared, coming towards them down the Concord River. At Nash's signal, a few members of his bodyguard upended a can of blue dye into the canal. There were still a few feet of water left in the canal at that spot, and the dye lazily drifted through the locks. The workmen down there uttered some colorful Gaelic curses as the vivid blue splashed on them, but they knew better than to complain.

As Nash had hoped, the Second backed away, avoiding the dye as it diffused into the river. Nash had planned for success: at his next signal, another barrel of dye was dumped into the river, a short distance upstream from the locks. The Second backed away further. A few more signals, and a few more barrels, and the spirit had been chased back to the mouth of Rivermeadow Brook, along Lawrence Street. At this point, the final stroke was made. The last dye barrel was dumped into the Concord, upstream of the creek mouth, so the Second had no choice but to retreat up the creek. A few more barrels sent It further up, past Hale's old sawmill on Central. At this point, four barrels were tipped over, but these were not opened, merely punctured, so that a steady drip would keep the creek polluted for days. Time enough for Nash to use his influence to get all the mills to dump their waste dye here, and anything else that was foul, nasty smelling and unnatural.

Nash gazed up the creek at the Second, now at bay. "How do you like that?" He shouted. "Do you like being imprisoned? You will never be able to roam free again! You can see the kind of influence I have over humans. Whatever you can persuade them to do, I can get ten times as many to undo it!"

Speaking of foul smells, Nash detected a distinctive odor from the tannery, just a few hundred feet away from where the dye barrels were dripping into the creek. Right along Tanner Street, of course. Nash could arrange for that operation to start dumping its waste in this direction: that should help in keeping that pesky spirit up the creek where it belonged.

It would be a simple matter for Nash to insure that this spot would remain a dumping ground for polluting industries of all kinds for many years to come. Of course, that would not be necessary, since now he could finish the job of preparing the way for the Master to escape, and it should all be over very soon…

It was fortunate that Nash was so focused on his contest with the Second that he hadn't noticed something odd near the Lower Locks: a dark-haired young woman appearing out of thin air, then fading away again.

It is usually unwise to try and interpret the thoughts of a Second in human terms, but it is reasonable to assume that Wamesit felt a degree of satisfaction as Its stratagem worked perfectly on that wounded Third. Naturally, the Third had assumed that this confrontation was all about him, about the exercise of his powers in the service of the Creature. It would not have occurred to him that this was a distraction, that the important part of this scene was the brief appearance and disappearance of the young woman a few yards upstream.

Wamesit knew Its Adversary, and the Adversary's servant, quite well. In the community of Seconds, Wamesit had become the expert on the creature imprisoned in the river. This had happened by accident. Centuries ago, the Second had decided to move north, as the practice of agriculture spread north on this continent. Someone would be needed to guide these people in the correct practices, as had been done with great success in Asia and Africa, and more recently South America and Europe. Establishing Its mentorship amongst the tribes who were beginning to take up the practice of settled agriculture, Wamesit discovered the horrible destructive being in the very midst of these humans. Soon enough Wamesit learned the truth: that this being had been recognized long ago as something extraordinarily dangerous, but impossible to destroy without unacceptable damage to the planet's capacity to support life. It had been dealt with in typical First fashion, slowly, with safeguards spanning uncounted millennia. Wamesit was the first of Its kind to become aware of the Demon, and quickly formed some conclusions of Its own. First, that It was not of this Earth.

Of a nature similar to the Firsts, but with capabilities, and certainly intentions, that were utterly unlike. Realizing this, Wamesit began to take a close interest in the Earth's surroundings in the galaxy. Its best eyes were those of humans, and on many cloudless evenings It watched the stars through these mortal instruments, richly rewarding those who cooperated most freely.

In the placement and motions of the stars was a message, as clear as it could possibly be. There was One who had an interest in this planet, in particular the world's vulnerability to the depredations of such as the Demon. The One had done something astonishing: bent spacetime to draw two time periods close enough that humans might pass from one to the other. The signs were there for those who could see them, but on this planet it was Wamesit alone who had thought to look. Knowing of the Demon, knowing of this special tool which could somehow be used against it, it was Wamesit's responsibility to motivate the humans who could answer not only this threat, but the broader one which its existence implied. And it was clear that only humans could do this. This was an interesting point of view. It was conventional wisdom among the Seconds that they were created to deal with the humans, as though they were some kind of plague (in the view of some Seconds) or as if they were dangerous imbeciles who would invariably do the worst thing imaginable at every turn if they were not meticulously guided away from such actions. Wamesit had seen some things, and understood some things, that other Seconds would never readily accept. Humans alone had the potential to safeguard the planet, to make it safe for all. Wamesit must select the most promising of the humans, and must give them the tools that they needed. Passaconaway had been a great success, as had Healey, but given the circumstances of their times and cultures they could only do so much. This one, who had made a brief but profoundly important appearance by the canal, while Wamesit was pretending to be chased off by a bunch of refuse, this human was the one to complete the task. Wamesit clearly recognized that she had come from a future time, and looked forward to meeting her when that time came…

Chapter 12

In which Beatrisa does some Unraveling

Present day: The sky was dark with thick, angry clouds. It had been raining heavily for days, and although it was not raining at the moment it looked like there was more to come. Puddles had formed at the edges of the streets, as the runoff was greater than the storm drains' capacity. There were hardly any cars on the street this morning.

A young woman walked along the sidewalk of Central Street, to the place where it crossed the Pawtucket Canal. She turned from the sidewalk, went down the steps to the scenic canal walkway, then lowered herself into the canal itself, where the water was chest deep. This would have caused some alarm, if there was anyone around to see, but there were no pedestrians on the street at the moment. The canal was a very slow-flowing waterway, but it was not unheard of for people to be found dead in the canals, of any of a number of causes.

Even if someone had called the police, nothing would have happened. The police and fire department, at this moment, were completely paralyzed. An inexplicable sit-in demonstration was happening outside every police and fire station in the city, apparently by a religious group called the "Church of the Divine Spirit". In particular, the demonstrators were blocking the driveways and garages so that none of the vehicles could move. No assistance could be expected from neighboring communities, either, since each of the incoming roads was blocked by two or more overturned trucks, all of which were labeled as carrying hazardous waste. There was apparently no attempt to hide the fact that this was all planned: even the highway and public works departments had their equipment yards blocked at the entrance by some of their own vehicles, with the tires slashed.

In the ominous quiet of the downtown scene, centered on the young woman standing in the center of the canal, it was easy to hear the first explosions in the distance…

> *1842: The sky was dark with thick, angry clouds. It had been raining heavily for days, and although it was not raining at the moment it looked like there was more to come. The streets were filling up with puddles, as the rainwater tried to find its circuitous way to the canal.*

There were hardly any carts or carriages on the street this morning.

A young woman walked along Central Street, to the place where it crossed the Pawtucket Canal. She turned from the street, climbed down to the canal side, then lowered herself into the canal itself, where the water was chest deep. This would have caused some alarm, if there was anyone around to see, but there were no pedestrians on the street at the moment. The canal was a very slow-flowing waterway, but it was not unheard of for people to be found dead in the canals, of any of a number of causes.

In the relative quiet, the young woman could easily hear the sound of rushing water in the distance...

Present day: Bea steadied herself in the cold, dirty canal water. She would have to be ready for water that was considerably deeper, and flowing considerably faster, very soon. She had spent the last two months preparing herself for this moment, but could not suppress her anxiety over the task she had taken on. Her first move, which involved placing herself physically and mentally in two different times at once, had gone smoothly enough. Fortunately, she could take the same steps down the same streets in both times, to get to this place. What was to follow would require close attention, fast reflexes, and perfect coordination between her two presences.

As she heard the sound of the first explosion, she knew that it was the Guard Locks being demolished. The river was at an unprecedented height above the falls, and the drop at the Guard Locks, normally only 2 feet, was now at least 6 feet, high enough to spill over the top of the upstream lock before it was demolished. There would be a tremendous, destructive turbulence, she knew, as the river tried to push its way through this newly cleared opening with a terrible force.

The second explosion, a few seconds later, was much closer. It came from the Swamp Locks, near the Park Service Visitors' Center. Bea imagined that these charges were probably arranged to clear the channel of the Pawtucket Canal, while blocking the branch canal entrances with debris, so that the flow would be concentrated toward the place where she was standing. From her place in the water, she looked up through the "industrial canyon", where the canal was lined by long mill buildings on either side. She could hear the growing roar of the flood water racing furiously through the channel. At the far end of the "canyon", she saw the water rise, and rise, and rise… impossibly high, three stories above street level. Logically, the first surge of floodwater, after making its way through the cleft between School Street Hill and the Highlands, would spread out and slow down at the broad plain around the Swamp Locks. But Bea knew that this water was obeying forces other than gravity.

The next explosion took her by surprise. These charges had been planted beneath the mill buildings themselves, and suddenly created a huge opening in the "canyon". At this point, the floodwater, which had raised itself unnaturally high, became something that was clearly alive, and terrifying in its ferocity. The shapes of enormous salamanders and sharks rose up in turn from the turbulence, to smash themselves against the remaining walls of the wrecked buildings, breaking them down even further. The forms changed as the water worked its way toward the place where Bea was standing. Watery shapes of huge reptiles which had not been seen on the Earth for over a hundred million years, came to savage, destructive life and continued the orgy of demolition. Sometimes it was a form that was almost human, but gigantic in size, with heavy brows, a brutish expression and long, pointed teeth. No shape lasted more than a few seconds before subsiding into the rushing water and being replaced by a form equally savage and violent. It did not seem to take any special notice of Bea in its efforts to widen its path, but it was frightening enough nonetheless. As it drew closer to her, the form of a huge sledgehammer rose from the water, and came down repeatedly, smashing the low bridge where Central Street crossed the canal. The water where Bea was standing had been gradually rising, and was up to her chin at this point A chunk of concrete from the bridge flew by, narrowly missing her.

Now the flood was upon her. In a fraction of a second, the living flood, holding a shape in defiance of gravity, rushed forward and enveloped her.

> *1842: The river was at an unprecedented height above the falls. This would not normally be a matter of great concern, as the canal system had been engineered*

with elaborate safeguards. It would take an extraordinary set of coincidental errors, extraordinary carelessness on the part of many different people, or numerous acts of bold, coordinated sabotage to make the system fail.

Moss stood above the Guard Locks. Looking down, he saw that on the low side there was hardly any water: the canal appeared drained. And it was so, since he himself had just opened all of the downstream locks, one by one, before coming here. Ordinarily he would have met with considerable resistance from the lock tenders, who would not have permitted such dangerous actions, even by someone who was in a position of authority over them. But this day, every single one of the lock tenders had come down with a mysterious illness, with vomiting, diarrhea, crippling headaches and vertigo, leaving the lock stations deserted. It was a simple matter for Moss to open the Lower Locks, then the Swamp Locks, and let all the water presently in the canal find its way to the Concord River and thus back into the Merrimack.

With such a height of water behind the Guard Locks, it was a bit more perilous to open that one. But Moss had prepared for this in previous weeks, by gradually working loose the clamps holding the hinges on which the locks swung. A few blows with a sledgehammer was all it took to release one side of the lock at the top, so that it sagged inward under the pressure of the upstream water, snapped the hinge on the bottom, and fell into the channel. With the water rushing in, the other side of the lock could not hold, and fell away in a few seconds.

Moss felt a sense of elation as the floodwater rushed to fill the channel, higher and higher. He could feel the spirit of the Master pouring in from the river into the canal. Soon, very soon, the water would carve out a channel wide enough to carry It to the river, well downstream from the falls, and out to the ocean after untold eons of imprisonment. It was not enough simply to know. He had worked so diligently, and cleverly, to make this happen, and wanted to see all of it. He ran up to a safe height, then followed the path of the canal to the industrial area. Watching from the vantage point of the railroad terminal, he saw the giant, monstrous shapes, shapes of ancient creatures, and other things that never existed on Earth, rise from the water, smash against the canal walls and the mills on either side, and fall back into the water, to be replaced by other shapes. As the path of destruction moved toward Central Street and the Lower Locks, he again ran to follow it and enjoy the spectacle. From the Lower Locks, he just barely noticed the figure of a young woman standing in the middle of the canal as the flood's unnatural fury approached her....

Bea kept her composure as the flood enveloped her in both times. She had to wait for the right moment, when the creature was sufficiently present, sufficiently concentrated in this spot. She knew that in her time there was supposed to be one more explosion, at the Lower Locks immediately behind her. But this would not happen, because Rudy and Professor O'Malley had found and disconnected that charge earlier this morning. This meant that the flood, animated with the gathering presence of the Demon, would be temporarily stopped here.

> *1842: Earlier this morning, Charles Healey and Tin had carted in some Irish stone, which had been held in reserve, to the Lower Locks, where they were added to the canal lining just short of the lock mechanism. They also closed the locks here, which Moss had left open. They had had to work quickly and quietly to avoid being noticed prematurely by Moss. The result was that the floodwaters conveying the Demon would be held up at this spot.*

She had to be patient, waiting for the creature to gather itself here. She could feel Its power and malice building up by the second. When she sensed that It was fully present, she opened her mind and took hold of the watery Demon. With a single awareness in both time periods, she could do this with perfect coordination.

The creature, distracted and frustrated by these unexpected blockages, turned Its attention on Bea. This was her opportunity: she could now visualize the being, Its pattern, the way It controlled the motion of the water, and she could grasp this firmly in her mind, as she had been mastering the manipulation of solid objects and of currents in the air and water. She held her grip on the creature, in both times, and tried to ignore the sensations It was filling her mind with, first of falling, then of burning, then of being crushed by boulders, then of being ripped apart by savage animals. Then other sensations, more disturbing, scenes of torture inflicted on helpless animals, on children, by Bea herself. As disturbing as these impressions were, they seemed oddly impersonal, as though they were being directed at her in some reflexive fashion, without any real awareness or personal malice. Bea fought to exclude them from her attention.

The thing in the water, before Its imprisonment, had done a great deal of killing. It began with the great Cambrian Extinction, the sudden and mysterious disappearance of more than half the species in the fossil record some 400 million years ago. Since Its entrapment in this place, It had developed a little more finesse, attempting to seize control of the minds of living creatures to force them to do its bidding. More often than not, this killed them outright, but it didn't matter since there was an unlimited supply of creatures to replace them. It was quite an unusual exercise in subtlety, however, for the creature to resort to intimidation, but this is what It now attempted. In the contact between Its mind and Beatrisa's It showed her a vision of all the living things which It had killed over the many millions of years in this place. Millions of animal species supplied It with victims: their bodies contributing to the rich soil along the riverbanks. In more recent years, many human beings had been killed as well. Bea was forced to see each one, understand who they were, and experience their confusion, panic and pain as the creature idly took their lives. People from cultures undiscovered by archeologists; people from the nations that lived here at the time of European contact; fur traders, explorers, farmers, workers, soldiers, children, drunks and criminals: all dragged under the water to join the ghastly community of corpses at the river bottom.

This was subtlety and focus beyond the creature's normal capability. Beatrisa was dismayed, horrified, disgusted, filled with sorrow at the truncated lives and the pain, but her purpose was not affected. The creature sensed this, and sensed that she had a grip that would not allow It to pass by this spot unless It dealt with her. One thing which the creature was well practiced in was drowning people, so It decided that this was what It must do. The water gathered at this spot, by the Lower Locks, swelled into a sphere, expanding larger and larger, forty, fifty, sixty feet in diameter, filling the space between the hotel and the old Sun building, pressing against the windows on both sides. No human being in the creature's experience could remain alive very long under so much water.

It seemed as though the drowning must have worked, because the human's grip was released. And miraculously, the blockages that had been in place just beyond where the human stood were also gone. An opening appeared though which the creature was able to pass… And on the other side, was a more suitable victim, not a puny human or other fleshy organism but a being of a type similar to Itself, probably one of Those who had imprisoned It so long ago. Fulfilling Its long-delayed destiny, It attacked with all Its fury…

With all of her strength and breath gone, Beatrisa pushed herself hard to the surface of the water, took a gasping breath, made her way out of the water, over the wall and onto the walkway. She could sense that the creature had used the opening that she had created, had seen Itself on the other side, and was now fully engaged in devouring Itself. To be more precise, the creature in 1842 was attacking the one in the present, and vice versa, both trapped in an eternal loop of self-destruction.

The Demon in the present began to fade and diminish as It became further engaged in this titanic battle with Its other self through the time portal. In a few seconds, all of Its visible manifestations had vanished. It was gone.

At a safe distance, she turned to look. The violence was over as abruptly as it had begun: no more agitated shapes in the water, no more destruction, just a whirlpool which was gradually slowing down and disappearing. Bea collapsed on the ground. It was at this point that she withdrew her "presence" from the earlier time. It felt as though the passage, the "thin spot" between the two times, was fading away as she did so.

O'Malley and Rudy Foster came running up to help her. When her breath returned, she told them, "It's done. The Demon will now spend eternity destroying Itself between the years 1842 and this day. It likes to unravel things: now It can unravel Itself. From this moment forward It does not exist in this universe." Both men seemed sobered by the news. Rudy said, "Bea, you have done what the Gods could not, and now the world has changed.

How much of the character of life on earth, and of our human existence, has been driven by the tension of this being's imprisonment? And what is to come in this new age? I wonder."

Chapter 13

In which Beatrisa receives a very old Note, and the Other Shoe is Dropped

The clouds were breaking up, but there was still water everywhere. Thankfully, it was water of the familiar, tame variety, not the sort that was likely to reach out and grab you. The few people wandering around the downtown streets looked dazed and aimless, torn between a curiosity over the explosions and strange crashing floodwater, and fear over what might happen next. Bea was soaking wet, and needed to go home for a change of clothes and a rest. She had agreed to meet Rudy and O'Malley later on at the churrascario near Chapel Hill to discuss what they should all do next.

At home, showered, dressed and feeling refreshed, Bea headed into the kitchen, where she saw a note on the table. It hadn't been there when she had first gotten home. And, even odder, it was on a sheet of paper yellowed with age, as though it had been sitting right there on the table for the last hundred and sixty years or more.

As she started reading, she realized that it was a note from Tin:

"Dear Beatrisa,

Words are inadequate to express appreciation for your accomplishment. The community of life on Earth owes you its deepest gratitude, though it may be a long time before your actions become widely known. I will now remain in my time, your past, content in the knowledge that the creature, though still with us, is doomed.

It is a comfort to me that the passage between the times, which made this possible, has disappeared. Although it was necessary to meet this dire crisis, and we used it with the utmost care to avoid paradoxes, its existence troubles me greatly, and I will maintain the hope that such manipulations of the fabric of the universe will not occur again in my lifetime. Make no mistake, the possibility of travel through time is a spiritual matter of the greatest consequence. If our actions, our experiences, and our very existence, can be undone or changed, then our existence is without meaning and there can be no purpose in anything that we do. This is a matter of faith, perhaps the most basic: I must believe that the universe is real, and that the path of our action and experience is unique.

You will no doubt be wondering, now that this crisis is past, what it is that you are to do with the rest of your life. I strongly recommend that you seek out the Bashaba for advice in the matter, for your work is far from done. I believe that he hinted at this in your earlier encounter, but you were understandably able only to attend to the immediate issue. It is now essential that you understand these things. He is ready, and anxious, to speak with you.

If we are to meet again in your time, then it will be because I arrived there in a decent and wholesome manner, having experienced the full span of the intervening years. Life is full of uncertainty, with or without demons, but I hope that this will come to pass.

Very truly yours,

Tin"

Bea left the apartment, which in her mind was now filled with delightful echoes of Margaret Conlon, and met with her two conspirators over a well-earned 'rodizio' dinner. Since they had been out and about in the meantime, they filled her in on recent events. The city was slowly drawing itself back to normal. The overturned trucks had been cleared away, and the demonstrators had been picked up and, temporarily, jailed in various neighboring communities, since there was not room enough in the city jail for all of them. They turned out to be a cooperative bunch for the most part, most of them seeming a bit confused and embarrassed over participating in what was clearly an utterly pointless act of civil disobedience. Their messiah, "Father Oswald" had also been picked up for observation when he was seen wading into the river, shouting, "Hold me up! Hold me up!"

"Any news of the City Hall Third?" asked Bea. "Not really", replied Rudy. "We took a look at 'Wilkins' office, and there was no one there. I don't think anybody knows what happens to a Third when it is released from this kind of possession: this is a case without precedent. Does it die? Does it realize the error of its ways and become consumed with guilt? Does it go mad and continue to serve a master that no longer exists? We could always ask the Professor, here, to use his Sight and track down the miserable creature. But your batteries have been drained enough lately, haven't they?" They all laughed, half-heartedly.

"Thank you for your concern", replied O'Malley, "and you are right. As thrilling as it is to use the Sight, it makes me feel like an old-style flashbulb. You know, one shot and it's spent. What I have 'seen' so far has given me a lifetime of things to think about and investigate, and I am content to leave that capability for when it is really needed. I would also like to know what happened to Moss, but I have a feeling we will find out sooner or later."

"And what about you, Bea?" asked Rudy. "After what we have all seen, and what you have done, it's hard to see what kind of normal life you could feel comfortable about going back to. I will keep the shop open for as long as you want to keep doing that work, but I do not expect that you will want to for very long."

"There is someone I need to talk with about that" replied Bea. "We have all been through some amazing things, and I have opened doors which can not be closed again. I have been told that there are still some very important things that I must do, and I don't doubt that, but I have no idea what they are. I will tell you one thing: I have become very intolerant of foolish obstacles. For instance, I still don't have a green card, or a damned Social Security number. Somehow that isn't as dispiriting as it used to be, but it still annoys me when I think of it."

The next morning, Bea took the car and drove up along the river to Tyngsborough. Without any difficulty she located the dirt road off the highway which led to the island that "wasn't there". But, as it was for Tin and Healey in 1842, the island was "there" for Bea now. She stepped across the short causeway and up the path.

Passaconaway was sitting in front of his house, as he had been on the previous visit. It was as if no time had passed at all. Perhaps, here, that was actually true. He rose to greet her.

“Welcome and congratulations, young Warrior”, he said. “I surmise, from the fact that you have returned here, that the Beast has been destroyed.”

“It has” she replied. “It is eternally devouring Itself during the period from 1842 to a point in time a few hours ago.”

“A fitting end, and a new life for the planet” said Passaconaway. “And now I can join my ancestors without shame”.

“Shame? I don’t understand”

“In my lifetime, I was responsible for a great nation of people. Innocent people, who deserved the full measure of my abilities to protect them from harm. But as events unfolded, an even greater responsibility came upon me, to safeguard the world for all of life to come. It required a terrible compromise. I sacrificed the well-being of my people in the service of this greater task. The choice has weighed heavily on my heart. But with this successful outcome, my choice has been vindicated, and my burden is lifted.

“Your heroism merits the thanks of the Gods, although there is only one among them who fully appreciates it. Aside from the Gods, in my opinion, the Old Ones expected this of you from the beginning, so it is not reasonable to expect their gratitude. As you must be aware, you have now within you the means to gain whatever your heart desires, to defeat any foe, to overcome any difficulty, to accomplish miracles that ordinary people could scarcely comprehend. At this moment, the thing that you need the most is a gift that is mine to bestow: a purpose for your life. And it is simply this: though I could not protect my people, you can and must protect yours.

"My people? What do you mean?"

"You know what I mean. I see the unease in your heart. It is not the fact that you must live in the shadows in this country because of the manner in which you arrived here. You clearly have the power to surmount such petty personal inconveniences. No, it is the fact that those that you love and cherish, all of your countrymen, suffer the same way, and are not strong as you are. You feel that you do not belong with them. You feel that there is nothing you can do to help them. You are wrong. Find a way to help them, and you will find the solution for yourself. You are more fortunate than I was" he said, "because your path is straight. Each action that you take will serve every one of your purposes, even those which you must yet discover. Ponder this question, if you will: where did the Demon come from?"

As she walked back across the causeway, the island faded from view, and once she was across, the causeway disappeared as well, leaving only an overgrown dirt track that appeared to lead right up to a weedy riverbank. She thought about this as she drove back home. This trick I pulled on the Demon, what use is that for helping people get green cards? It doesn't make sense.

But suddenly, it all made a great deal of sense. As before, Passaconaway's words opened a door in her mind. And what was revealed was so overwhelming that Bea had to stop the car by the side of the road, and fully digest this new understanding. Of course there was a way to help her countrymen here. It was elaborate, and would take time, but it was well within her capabilities, and it would definitely work. But that was not all: in fact it was only the beginning of something much, much greater. It suddenly became obvious to Bea that although Earth had been saved from a terrible threat in its midst, there was still a great danger looming, from another direction entirely. In a flash, she could clearly visualize the threat, and what she would have to do about it. It would require a project of great complexity, involving many people in places all over the world, and would stretch her newfound capabilities to the limit. But miraculously, there was no conflict between this and her desire to help her friends and neighbors: her efforts to improve the condition of her fellow undocumented immigrants would become the foundation of the greater project. And her special computer programs, which she had been pursuing as a hobby at Rudy's shop, were a vital tool that she needed to begin this mission, and would have a central role in protecting the world from these other threats. It all made sense, it was all urgently necessary, and she knew exactly how to do it. And it would utterly change the terms under which humans shared the planet, and this region of space, with other forms of life. After that, the real, important work could begin. Passaconaway was right: her path was clearly laid out before her, leading, step by inevitable step, from a rundown apartment building on the slopes of Chapel Hill, to someplace light-years from Earth.

Once again driving back home, daring to cross the Merrimack at the Rourke Bridge for the first time in years, she smiled as she contemplated how this work would begin. It would require a bit of drama, to get people's attention…

Chapter 14

In which Beatrisa kicks Ass, and Moss takes Time Out

Beatrisa walked through the front door into the narrow foyer of the small apartment building. It was freezing cold in here, hardly any better than being outside, now that it was the middle of January. The landlord's apartment was the first one on the left. She saw the sign on the door "Gordon – Building Manager". She knocked on the door, loudly, three times. As the door opened, a flood of warm air, heavy with cigar smoke, poured into the hallway. This was probably the only apartment in the building with heat. The man standing in the doorway was very tall and broad-shouldered, although his gut was considerably bigger. No doubt he had been an athlete of some sort, decades in the past, and he retained an air of confidence in his ability to intimidate people with his size. "What do you want?" he demanded, in a voice dripping with scorn. He shot a quick glance upward, since apartment doors were opening all over the building, and tenants were sheepishly approaching the stairwell for a look. The word had been passed around earlier, that something exceptional was going to happen.

After waiting a few seconds for her audience to collect, Bea made her speech, in a voice which could be heard all through the building:

"James Gordon, my name is Beatrisa DeSouza. It has come to my attention that you have been mistreating the tenants of this building. You are not providing heat or hot water in the coldest part of winter. You do not perform the repairs that are your responsibility. You have taken rent from people for six months in advance and then evicted them. You raise the rent capriciously, and threaten to call ICE when people complain. You use the same threat to try to extort sexual favors from the young women who live here. You have used your fists to beat older women and children who live here. You must change this pattern of behavior, or face the consequences. I will hear your choice now."

At first, the man chuckled. He was genuinely amused that this tiny little Brazilian girl thought she could tell him what to do with his own property. But he was accustomed to thinking of himself as refined and sophisticated (despite overwhelming evidence to the contrary), so he tried to dismiss her in what he thought was a dignified manner.

“Miss DeSouza, these people are liars, and I think you know that better than I do. Whatever it was you hoped to accomplish here, you’ve been very brave, and I applaud you, but now it’s time to run back home to Mama.”

Bea drew herself up as tall as she could manage. “I will have your answer NOW!!” she thundered, and her voice actually made doors and windows rattle. It rattled Gordon as well, and he forgot all about his attempt to appear respectable.

“Okay, little girl, I think it’s time to remind these people of how things really are...”

He was quick, no doubt about it. Under normal circumstances his huge meaty fist would have struck her jaw before she had time to react. Of course, from Bea’s perspective, the man was moving in slow motion. She stood her ground, but briefly phased herself, so that his fist went right through where her head appeared to be. Then, to Gordon’s surprise, and everyone else’s as well, he could not draw his arm back: it appeared to be stuck, as though it was embedded in an invisible block of concrete suspended in midair. Bea patiently allowed him to vainly struggle to pull his hand free, providing a comical pantomime for the rapt crowd. Finally, with the stage properly set, Bea delivered her coup. Once again, in a loud, clear voice, audible throughout the building, she said to Gordon:

"You have chosen unwisely, and your life is now mine to do with as I please. Know now, that as of this moment, every bank account, credit account, or account of any other kind in your name, has vanished without a trace. Your driver's license and social security number have suddenly become invalid. You cannot make a call from your cell phone, you cannot cash a check, and you cannot withdraw money from an ATM. This building now belongs to the Orixa Corporation…"

This drew a muffled gasp from some of the older tenants, who knew what that name implied. Some crossed themselves, but no one looked away.

"…and any inspection of the property tax records will show that it has belonged to the Orixa Corporation, and not to you, for the last two years. You are neither an owner nor a tenant in this building: you are a squatter, or worse. Accordingly, a call has been placed to the police. When they arrive, they will find a large number of unregistered handguns and a large quantity of cocaine in your apartment, bearing your fingerprints and no one else's. And, of course, you are now an undocumented person. Maybe ICE will take an interest. Do you think so?

"Now, for your immediate future. You will remain stuck like this for 15 minutes after I leave. From then until the time the police arrive, you will be unable to speak or to leave this building, or to touch or move the incriminating evidence in your apartment. Your keys will not work on any apartment door but your own.

"After your arrest, I think you will agree that without any cash or credit, or any verifiable identity, it is unlikely that you will make bail, or be able to obtain a good lawyer for your defense. You have done all this to yourself, and I am simply the instrument."

Bea then turned to the stairwell, and repeated the essence of this speech in Portguese to the stunned onlookers, adding:

"This building now belongs to me, which means that it belongs to you. We will work out the arrangements at a later time. In return I ask several things of you. First, stay in your apartments and do not harm this man until the police remove him. I guarantee that his hurt and humiliation will be everything you could want, and more besides. You will not see him here again.

"Second, tell everyone what has happened here. Tell your friends, your neighbors, your families. Some of you know where to find me. Let others know: oppression and exploitation of our people will no longer be tolerated.

"Third, once we have cleaned the filth from Gordon's apartment, we will use it to hold free classes in English, in mathematics, in business, and law. You will help me with this. Good night to you all. Oh, and by the way, after the police have left, someone should go to the basement and turn up the heat."

With that, Bea turned away from the silent crowd, went outside and fetched the large satchel which she had left on the front step. She opened it, and holding the guns and plastic bags with gloved hands, pressed them against Gordon's helplessly stuck fingers to place his fingerprints on them. She went into his apartment and carefully arranged them on his kitchen table, whistling a happy song that she had learned from her mother. As she passed Gordon on her way out, she leaned towards him and whispered, "I made this look like a choice, but I knew full well you had no choice. Your meanness and stupidity forced you to react as you did, which was exactly what I wanted from you. You deserve everything that will happen to you, but you should know that I used you to serve as a demonstration of my power to the community. I thank you for your unwitting cooperation, for holding true to your brutish nature this one last time. In return for this favor, I give you the gift of knowledge, which is both Heaven and Hell." She touched his forehead lightly with a forefinger. The man's eyes went wide, his expression softened, and his jaw dropped. Bea continued, "I will visit you in one week's time, to discuss your thoughts regarding your actions, and mine. I will be sincerely interested in what you have to say".

Bea had already turned and walked out the front door as tears of shame and regret began coursing down the big man's face. She made her way up the sidewalk at a relaxed pace, although she still had much yet to do this evening. So many tasks, of many different kinds, desperately needed to be done, today, tomorrow and for years to come. She would accomplish many profoundly significant and satisfying goals along the way, but all of this, even what she had done earlier this year in the canals of Lowell, was ultimately devoted to a single purpose, one that was utterly obvious now that Passaconaway had brought it to her attention.

She turned to walk up the short side street to her home. Approaching sirens could be heard in the distance.

****

The bitter January wind blew the drifted snow sideways, stinging his face. Moss looked down at the ground ahead of him, looking neither to the right nor to the left as he trudged along the side of the road. He walked slowly, with a shuffling gait, as most of his energy was devoted to his concealment spell. He could not bear the thought of contact of any kind with humans, who at this moment seemed so superior to him in their innocence. Rationalizations, excuses and self-delusion were not an option for his kind, and he had no choice but to face the bare truth of the things he had done for so many years. He remembered everything: his early years helping the Seconds guide the Incas, his journey north, and that horrible unexpected discovery that awaited him in New England, the brutal injury to his mind which, tragically, had not killed him outright.

At a spot which he remembered from so long ago, he turned from the road and shuffled down an overgrown dirt path through a small patch of trees. The path appeared to end abruptly at a lazy, marshy backwater of the river, but Moss stepped with confidence onto what appeared to be empty air. The causeway appeared as his foot landed upon it, and he walked across to the island that had also not been visible a moment ago. Here, it was a pleasantly warm sunny day, probably in mid-June. A pleasant breeze bore the scent of wildflowers. The bleak winter landscape was nowhere to be seen.

Moss followed the path up the hill. There was no one else on the island, but there was an iron pot filled with a stew of fish and vegetables, hanging over a small fire. It smelled wonderful. Moss sat down on the wooden bench outside the modest log cabin. Here, outside the flow of time, isolated from the world in which he had failed in his duty so completely, he would sit alone, and contemplate the events which had transpired since he set foot on this continent over three centuries ago. He would consider every hurtful thing that he had done, the large and the small, the direct and the indirect, the intentional and the unintentional. Until he had fully considered every act and its consequences, and found a way to come to terms with it, and a way, somehow, to make it right, he would not allow himself to reenter the world. If he was not sure of himself, if he could not fully trust himself, if he did not understand his limitations, he would be a sentient being without purpose. Killing himself would be extraordinarily difficult, and would not solve the problem in any case. So here he would sit, and remember, and think, as long as it took. Perhaps a thousand years. Probably more. It would be pointless to rush it.

Appendix: Lowell Chronology

This story includes many references to actual places, historical events and people. The following chronology will show how very little of this story was left to be "invented".

~400 Million BC

Sudden mass extinction of the majority of living species on Earth. The Avalonian tectonic plate splits and the two sections drift apart. The eastern part now underlies Ireland, Britain, and a part of Portugal. The western part underlies eastern Massachusetts, Rhode Island, and parts of the Canadian Maritime Provinces. The boundary of the plate in Massachusetts can be traced in the course of various creeks and marshes, and in the course of the Merrimack River between Lowell and the Atlantic Ocean.

~9000 BC

Retreating ice sheet from the last Ice Age drags and drops immense clumps of debris, forming marshes, lakes and hills across New England. There is evidence that the Merrimack River had run directly from the bend at Lowell to Boston Harbor before the last Ice Age, and was diverted to its present course by mounds of debris (specifically,

School Street Hill and the Highlands) dropped by the receding ice sheet.

~500 – 1600 AD

Seasonal agricultural settlements along the Merrimack, including sites by Pawtucket Falls and the confluence with the Concord River.

1565 Birth of Passaconaway, the Bashaba (Emperor) of a large region of Southern New England. He gains a widespread reputation as a sorcerer who can "make water burn, rocks move and trees dance".

1620 English settlers land at Plymouth after a brief stay on Cape Cod.

1653 Town of Chelmsford founded: its territory included what later became the city of Lowell.

Missionary John Eliot petitions the Massachusetts General Court to set aside a portion of Chelmsford for the Wamesit "praying Indians". This land, by Pawtucket Falls, would later become the site of the City of Lowell.

1660 Passaconaway's farewell speech to the Wamesit.

1662 Massachusetts General Court grants Passaconaway a plot of land near the river in what is now Tyngsborough, to retire on.

1675 King Philip's War: wide-ranging but generally uncoordinated hostilities between indigenous peoples and settlers. During this time, a group of Chelmsford residents attack the peaceful Wamesit settlement in "retribution" for an attack by a totally unrelated tribe.

1686 With numbers dwindling, the Wamesit sell their land to Jonathan Tyng for a bargain price and move to Canada. Tyng sells the land in parcels to local farmers at a huge profit.

1792 – 1796

Pawtucket Canal is built to bypass the Pawtucket Falls, in order to transport logs from New Hampshire to shipyards at Newburyport. During the opening ceremonies, a barge carrying local dignitaries capsizes when the lock collapses. Many are frightened and embarrassed, but no one is killed or seriously injured.

1803 Middlesex Canal opens, connecting the Merrimack River above the falls directly to Boston Harbor. Logs can now be transported efficiently to Boston shipyards, in competition with Newburyport.

1815 Francis Cabot Lowell makes a tour of the textile mills in Lancashire, England. Although the mechanical designs are a closely guarded secret, Lowell commits his observations to memory and later reconstructs them in a pilot plant on the Charles River in Waltham. This is probably the single most effective act of industrial espionage in history.

1821 Members of the Boston Associates inspect Pawtucket Falls on the Merrimack River. Impressed with the 32-foot drop in the water level over the space of ½ mile, they decide on this as the site of their vastly expanded industrial complex.

1822 Hugh Cummiskey contracts with Boston Associates to supply Irish work gangs for canal construction.

1826 City of Lowell is incorporated. A network of power canals is built, using the original Pawtucket canal as its starting point, to supply power to a large number of textile mills which will spring up over the next 20 years.

1830s Slum area known as the "Paddy Camps" grows along the Western Canal, just outside the downtown area. There are two camps, one composed of Irish laborers from County Cork, and another with immigrants from Connaught. There are frequent hostilities between the two. Many Irish, in order to evade US entry fees, land in Canada and walk south into New England, and are the "illegal immigrants" of their time.

1831 St Patrick's Church is built, the first Catholic church in New England outside of Boston. It is located midway between the two "Paddy Camps" in the hope of quieting the hostilities between them. (Note: St. Patrick's, rebuilt in 1853, is still in its original location along the Western Canal).

1837 Kirk Boott dies in a carriage accident in downtown Lowell.

1852 Major flooding on the Merrimack. City is saved from serious damage by "Francis Gate", at the Guard Locks on the Pawtucket Canal. Designed by engineer James Francis, the large mechanism had previously been known as "Francis' Folly".

1850s and later

As textile companies strive to slash costs, "Mill Girls" are gradually replaced by immigrant labor, first Irish, then French Canadian, and later, from Portugal, Greece and other countries.

1876 Emperor Dom Pedro II of Brazil visits Lowell.

1920 – 1950

Textile industry declines and disappears from Lowell in the face of lower cost competition in the southern US and elsewhere. In most cases, mill buildings remain standing: owners cannot sell them, and cannot even afford to tear them down.

1977 Silresim Corporation declares bankruptcy and abandons its site on Tanner St by Rivermeadow Brook. Its facility is found to be leaking massive quantities of PCBs, dioxin, waste oil, solvents and heavy metals into the nearby groundwater. It is declared an EPA Superfund site in 1991, and reclamation activities are still ongoing.

1978 National Park Service establishes Lowell National Historical Park. This becomes the focal point for refurbishing old mill buildings for commercial and residential use all over the downtown area.

1990s Two major waves of immigration establish a presence in Lowell: from Cambodia and from Brazil. Brazilians initially settle in neighborhoods that have a remnant of the earlier Portuguese immigrant influence

Acknowledgments & Bibliography

A special thanks goes to Dorothy Langevin and Beverly Hoekstra for their excellent assistance in proofreading.

The best way to travel through time and experience Lowell's remarkable past is to visit the Park Visitors Center and take one of the guided tours. The National Park Service employees and volunteers do a wonderful job of bringing the early industrial period to life and making it real and understandable.

The following books were also very useful in illuminating the details of the early 19th century and other periods that have a bearing on this story:

Harriet Hanson Robinson, "Loom & Spindle or Life Among the Early Mill Girls", Press Pacifica 1976 (first published 1889).

Brian C. Mitchell, "The Paddy Camps: the Irish of Lowell 1821-61", University of Illinois Press 1988.

John Pendergast, "The Bend in the River", Merrimac River Press 1991.

Patrick M. Malone, "Canals and Industry: Engineering in Lowell 1821 – 1880", Lowell Museum 1983.

About the Author

Richard Hollman obtained his doctorate in Physics from Stanford University in 1983, and thereupon settled down to toil diligently in the electronics industry, which he continues to do. That work has apparently left him with a bit too much free time on his hands, which accounts for the present book, his first attempt at fiction, and at least two more to come very soon in the "Lowell Story" sequence.

11564825R00113

Made in the USA
Charleston, SC
06 March 2012